TAKING THE FORBIDDEN ROAD

Evelyn James is a retired school-teacher who has taught in Northern Ireland in both rural and urban communities. Her parents came from farming backgrounds in County Armagh and County Cavan.

Her first short story, 'The Garden of Eden', appeared in 'The Lady' magazine more than thirty years ago. Since then, she has written over two hundred short stories and articles which have been accepted for publication in Ireland, Britain and overseas, also radio scripts for the B.B.C. and Radio Eireann. 'Taking The Forbidden Road' is her first novel. Here she brings us a poignant love story, a story that could happen only in Ireland.

The Third House
Publishing

3 Victoria Road, Holywood, N. Ireland, BT18 9BA

First Edition   (Paperback) 1991
Copyright © Evelyn James 1991

ISBN 1 873758 00 6

Printed by Priory Press
Strand Avenue
Holywood
N. Ireland

TAKING THE FORBIDDEN ROAD

A Novel
by
Evelyn James

THE THIRD HOUSE
PUBLISHING

ONE

All the way back on the train from her sea-side holiday with Aunt Emily, Leah's thoughts kept swinging from heart-stopping day-dreams to moments of despair that such dreams might have no future. Leaving the small station, holding the brown fibre case that had once been her mother's, she watched other passengers disappear to their various homes. But Leah still felt far from ready to face her parents and tell them of the invitation she had received to go for a weekend to the country.

Beyond the mass of roof-tops came the hum of city life as she lingered by suburban gardens. A tree of ripening apples, motionless in the evening air, looked like a lovely painting; a bed of roses, orange-yellow with tints of red, seemed to have stolen their colours from the setting sun. Moving on, she nipped off a late sprig of lavender peeping through a fence, crushed it in her hand and inhaled the heady scent.

Everything beautiful matched the excitement that kept bursting within her. She smiled and touched the letter in her blazer pocket to make sure it was still there and safely out of sight. Then she caught her breath again on a stab of pain, knowing that her parents wished her to end the country visits to her school-friend, Muriel Linton.

Leah knew she should be grateful for the holiday she had just spent with Aunt Emily at the coast. She had her mother to thank for that as well as for all the weekends with Muriel. Her father had been against her going to the country right from the start. She had heard her mother almost pleading:

"After all, Matthew, for Leah to see something of life on a farm could be most educational - and in a nice way, too. Mrs. Dawson, our organist, used to know Muriel's people, especially the girl's

9

mother. She says Leah would be with a good religious family, in a nice wee Protestant village. They are not quite like ourselves, of course. But they might have her back in time for our own Sunday service."

All that and more had come to pass and now Leah could not bear to think those wonderful days were over. For more than two years - since she had been sixteen - she had been going to Muriel's for an occasional weekend and longer during holiday times. Then, just recently, even her mother had seemed to be against these visits, saying that now she and Muriel had left school, they would of course be going their separate ways.

This had happened after Muriel had told Leah's parents she hoped to be going away to attend an agricultural college in September to learn all about poultry-keeping and egg-production. She had added with her usual bright-eyed candour that, following this, she and her young farmer friend, Tom Coulter, were planning to get married.

"Well," Aunt Emily had said, when Leah told her, "I'm sure that marriage to a farmer is not quite the life your parents would want for you. They were both reared on a farm and knew it as quite a hard life. And you're certainly not so robust-looking as your young friend Muriel Linton I met last summer."

She had smiled appreciatively at Leah. "I'm not surprised, dear, they want to stop your country visits; you're quite the young lady since last I saw you." Leah had found herself blushing at this remark.

Aunt Emily was her mother's sister, a widow for several years whose two daughters, Jane and Carol, were married and away from home. She had written to Leah's parents during the summer saying she would be delighted to have Leah for as long as they could spare her.

Leah, listening anxiously at her bedroom door in their bungalow, had heard her mother say: "I think a little sea-air would do Leah good, Matthew, and get her ready for her new studies in September."

Leah had pictured her white-haired father, his slight frame bent over the small table at the sitting-room window, his very blue eyes raised from his Bible and all the surrounding notes and tracts - as he gave some thought to this weighty matter. Three years retired from managing a religious bookshop in the city, and more recently as a lay preacher in their little church, he now spent much of his time with Bible study, youth-work and any gardening he could manage with his sometimes stiff joints.

"Well - I suppose a change would do her good," her father said at length. "But you must warn her well, Margaret. You know your sister is not too careful about places she visits or the friends she chooses."

So, under her mother's watchful eye, Leah had packed her few things and tried to hide her sudden excitement at the thought of the coming freedom with her lively Aunt Emily.

"Remember, Leah," her mother had cautioned her, "you won't have me this time, and your aunt has her part-time office job to see to. You must be careful not to wander far on your own. And it would be better not to talk to strangers - especially men."

Leah had tried to look concerned. In the past she and her mother had made brief visits to see Aunt Emily, staying one or two nights only. Her father had never considered joining them on what he regarded as frivolous outings. And now that he was less active her mother rarely left him on his own.

Aunt Emily usually called to see them when she drove to the city. She was four years younger than Leah's mother, a bright, energetic woman of softer outline and less serious disposition. They were both of medium height with greying wavy hair that had once been a rich brown. Aunt Emily's had retained more of its original colour and she kept it short and smartly styled. Leah's mother pinned hers in a bun at the back or wore it in a plait round her head. Either way, it looked too heavy for her thin pale face. But Leah knew that was how her father wanted her to keep it.

"Now don't let your aunt talk you into visiting any Picture Houses or those so-called places of amusement," her mother told Leah before she left. "You know yourself what is right to do."

Yes, Leah knew only too well. Do nothing exciting.

Most of the girls at school had been to the Opera House, films, parties, real dances. Some had boy-friends. From the chatter in the cloak-room and her friendship with Muriel, Leah had already learned something of the outside world. She felt sorry for her parents boxed into their narrow little space - and trying to keep her there, too.

She wanted to experience more of this life for herself and, since the coming of the letter, the thought of returning to the country held an added wonder and excitement. As she walked on slowly homewards, she was already there. Sometimes she gave her case an extra swing on a renewed surge of hopeful anticipation that her parents would allow her at least one further visit.

Leah knew what was right and what was wrong according to God's Commandments. But the rules her parents kept to so rigidly - like no cooking or cleaning on Sundays and no listening to music other than hymns at anytime - were surely nothing more than petty observances?

She considered that 'Love thy neighbour as thyself' was more important and should include her great friend Helen and her family who lived quite near.

Sadly, Leah's father did not agree, and she was finding it increasingly difficult to understand her parents' way of life. As she recalled the past ten days with Aunt Emily she knew they would not have approved of many of the things she had done.

Some mornings, for the first time in her life, she had gone bathing with three young girls known to her aunt. Afterwards, they had hurried in great excitement to a nearby coffee-bar filled with appetising smells, lively chatter and music from a juke-box. While her companions responded with bright eyes and giggles to the light-hearted banter from some young men they knew, Leah remained nervous and unhappy, feeling she should not be there.

Aunt Emily was not like her parents. Free in the afternoons, she had walked with Leah along the beach or through the park. They visited shops and tea-rooms and on one occasion dined out in style. Leah's heart gave a sudden bound, for that was the day the invitation had come from the country. And this time it had not come from Muriel! Her aunt had taken her to a hotel that evening, but she had been so excited she could scarcely recall what meal she had eaten or what they had talked about.

When they were leaving, she had stopped suddenly at the foot of the stairway listening to the music of a waltz drifting into the foyer which reminded her of her previous visit to the country.

"Come on Miss Bright-Eyes," her aunt had said. "There's dancing in there tonight, and that's certainly not for you - if I know your parents!" She had given Leah a knowing smile. "Don't think

12

young lady that I haven't noticed you floating round the house to dance tunes on the wireless."

"That's something I can't do at home," Leah reminded her aunt as they walked on. "You know my parents listen only to the news, and even that is turned off if Father thinks it's unsuitable for me to hear."

"Don't worry, dear. I won't let you down," Aunt Emily had said.

But Leah knew this was far from being the whole story, and when they reached the house she had decided to confide in her aunt. She began with her very first visit to the country when Muriel and her brother Jim had taught her a few dances, like the waltz and the foxtrot, to have her ready for their next Young Farmers' Club hop. Even their parents, Mr and Mrs Linton, had joined in the fun with music from a gramophone in the big kitchen.

"I just couldn't tell them my parents would object," Leah said. "Muriel knows now how strict they are about certain things, and that I can't always agree with them. Since then, I've been to several Y.F.C. dances. You see, Aunt Emily, I love music and dancing."

Her aunt had made a little whistling sound. Then she shook her head.

"Oh, Leah, just think what your parents would say about that!"

"I daren't tell them; they'd kill me; they think dancing is wicked. I always told them about the work being done on the farm, the church services I sometimes attended, village concerts, sales and flower-shows. They always assumed there was nothing else. And I feel so guilty. Now, as I told you, they don't want me to go back. They say Muriel and I will have little in common in the future."

"Well, then," her aunt had said, "there's no real harm done, is there? I'm sure the pair of you can meet again somewhere else later on."

"Oh, but I must go back!" Leah's voice had risen anxiously. "You see I've had an invitation from the country today. And if they stop me going it will break my heart."

"So - your heart is involved, Leah?" Her aunt had smiled kindly.

"Well, I don't really know." Leah's heart with its quickening beat seemed to have no such doubts.

"It's Muriel's brother Jim you like, I suppose?"

Leah shook her head. "No, a friend of the Lintons called Ray

Anderson. He and Jim were at the village school together. Now they are both twenty-one. The invitation I got this morning came from Ray as Muriel is on holiday. I like Ray very much, Aunt Emily, and sometimes I think he likes me. My mother questioned me a lot about Muriel's brother Jim and I told her I rarely saw him except at mealtimes, which was not exactly true. I couldn't possibly mention Ray - with parents like mine."

"Well - don't do anything foolish, Leah," her aunt had advised. "If you see this young man Ray again, I think you should confide in your mother. I feel sure she would understand."

"She's not like you," Leah told her aunt. "I sometimes think she would like to be. But then there's Father."

Her aunt had nodded. "Yes, your mother and I got on well in the old days. We still do in many ways. We used to work hard on the farm, but there were social events as well - parties, concerts, dances - oh, yes, Leah, you needn't look so surprised. Your mother loved dancing, too. It was when she met your father that she accepted his very strict, self-denying life-style. Your parents are good-living, sincere people who think the world of you and are always considering your welfare. Remember that, Leah."

Leah was now passing the small park near her home. She sighed deeply and sank on to the nearest seat, thinking how difficult it was sometimes to talk to her parents. How could she bear it if they refused to let her return to the country? So many of the things she liked to do were considered wrong in their eyes. They had also stopped her visiting the home of her friend, Helen Burke, whom she had met on the bus going to school.

When her father had heard that Helen attended a Convent school, he had stopped her visits. "Do your talking on the bus and make it brief," he had said harshly. "Just remember that this girl's upbringing as a Roman Catholic is totally unacceptable to us and makes her an unsuitable friend for you." Leah had never before seen her father so angry.

Aunt Emily, when she had heard this, had nodded gravely. "Well, now, Leah, your father has very strong views about mixed marriages - I mean Protestants marrying Catholics. And Helen, you say, has two older brothers. Your father's own sister married a Catholic called Sean Garvey, and this brought nothing but unhappiness and division to the two families concerned. Yet, previously, they had been quite friendly, even helpful towards each other on their adjacent farms. But as each child of the marriage was baptised into the Catholic faith so bitterness and enmity between them increased. Your grandparents had hoped that the girls, at least, would be brought up as Protestants and so keep a link between the two families."

Leah had listened with interest to this family story that was new to her.

"Your father," Aunt Emily went on, "was the younger son and later on he left the farm and began his new work in the city. After their parents' deaths, inside the same year, the home place was sold privately to a Protestant neighbour. Your father and his brother had known that their Catholic relations, having three sons, were most anxious to acquire their mother's home and land. But they were never given the chance."

Leah said that it seemed crazy to spoil the lives of so many people all over disagreement about religious practices. It made no sense. But her aunt had told her there was more to it than that; it was a rift between two peoples that went back hundreds of years. Yet in spite of this, most members of the two religious groups managed to live quite amicably and had many interests in common.

"And you and Mother - where were you at this time?" Leah had asked.

"I came here to an office job in this sea-side town, married and stayed. Your mother studied music and taught in the city. She met your father at Bible meetings and later joined his little church. As you know, after her marriage, she was their organist until they both retired. When our parents died, the small farm was sold. The few hundreds we received for it helped to pay off both our present homes. When you were born, your mother was nearly forty and your father fifty. Your coming was both a shock and a delight to them and since then their lives have revolved around you, but their strong, religious convictions have never changed."

Leah's meditations were suddenly interrupted by the sight of a black cat approaching her seat, walking jauntily. It brushed her legs with a friendly mew and then went on. Could this be a lucky omen? On a new wave of hope, she glanced around and then withdrew from her pocket a folded sheet of note-paper. She knew every word of the message but could not resist another peep at the firm, regular writing in deep blue ink that made her heart race as she read:

Dear Leah,

The Y.F.C. hope to have a social evening next Friday before Muriel leaves for her College. She is still away on holiday and not aware of our plans. Mrs Linton gave me your address and hopes you will be home in time. So do I. She says Muriel will call for you as usual that afternoon. I do hope you can come, Leah. I am looking forward to seeing you again.

Ray.

After carefully replacing the letter, Leah lifted her case and moved on. As she turned into her own avenue she was still picturing Ray, seeing his dark eyes lighting up as he came to claim her for a dance in the village hall. She was completely happy when he was about, and usually he treated her with great friendliness. There were other times, she had to admit, when he seemed to retreat from her, and she could sense almost a sadness in him. She told herself that this was understandable, for Muriel had said he had become a very serious young man having the care of family and farm following his father's death in a motor accident less than a year before Leah had met him.

Suddenly, she was jerked back to the present by someone waving from a front garden across the road. "Leah! I got your card. We've been to Roundstone in County Galway, just back yesterday. The boys are still away camping."

Leah's eyes widened in admiration as she recognised her friend, Helen Burke, looking nicely tanned and minus her pigtails and school uniform. She was wearing a green pleated skirt and flowered blouse and smiling a little self-consciously under her new dark helmet of cropped hair.

"You look great!" Leah called as she moved towards her. "All set for the Teacher Training College, I suppose?"

Helen nodded. "Yes, I'm really looking forward to going." She reached out and touched Leah's blonde curls that brushed her shoulders.

"You've had it cut, surely," she said in some surprise. "And I like the centre parting and your two gold clips."

"Thank you," Leah said. "The clips were a present from Aunt

Emily and my mother allowed me to have my hair trimmed to keep it healthy. So I took the opportunity to have three or four inches off!" They both laughed.

"I suppose it will be shorthand and typing for you very soon," Helen said.

Leah nodded, more serious now. "As you know, I'm not all that keen. But my father would like to see me working for his old firm or some other religious establishment."

"Well, I'm glad you're back, Leah. Judith will be sixteen on Friday and we'd love you to come to her party. You haven't called with us for ages."

Leah felt a tightening inside her as she recalled how her father had put a stop to those happy times with Helen's lively family: her two young sisters, Judith and Fran; brothers Paul and Damien attending the University; her busy welcoming parents.

Memories came flying: the girls in green and gold costumes practising their Irish dancing while Paul played the violin; Helen at the piano, her fingers flying over the notes of 'The Kerry Dancing' while they all sang the words so joyously.

At home, Leah had her mother's small harmonium on which she often played her favourite hymns. No other form of music was allowed in the house.

And many hymns were an inspiration and a delight. Yet Leah knew there was other wonderful music that, in some mysterious way, could reach her very soul, music that was full of dreams and all the beauty of the world. How could it be wrong, how could it be sinful, to play such music, to sing or to dance to it?

"Oh, Helen," Leah said, with real regret, "I don't think it will be possible. I have just heard that my friend, Muriel, hopes to call for me on Friday. But please give my best wishes to Judith. I'll see you later. Now I have to go or my parents will think I have missed the train.

TWO

As Leah entered her own garden, she noticed the harlequin standard-rose, its multi-coloured blooms gracing the centre flower-bed. Her own favourite Peace roses above clumps of French marigolds neatly bordered the drive.

Then the hall door opened and her mother appeared. She was wearing her usual brown skirt, but now with the new cream blouse she had been making for herself when Leah had left.

"You're looking very smart," Leah told her.

"And you're looking well improved," her mother said. "But Leah your hair - what have you had done to it?"

"Don't worry, Mother - it will soon grow."

Her father stood frowning in the hallway. "Your aunt's interference, as usual, I suppose. You're very late, Leah; we've been worried."

No outward show of affection came from her parents. That was their way. It was different in Muriel's home. Mrs Linton often gave Leah a quick hug on arrival or to show appreciation for something she had said or done.

"I was talking to Helen for a minute or two," she said. "They're just back from the west coast and - "

Her father had turned away sharply and she felt again the barrier that was growing between them, a feeling that saddened her often these days.

A card from Muriel was on the mantelpiece - a view of the lough near her uncle's farm in County Fermanagh. She read it quickly, noting that her friend would be home the following day. The card she herself had sent to her parents mentioned the good weather and Aunt Emily's fine crop of runner-beans and onions.

"You didn't tell us much of what you were doing," her father

18

remarked, watching her closely.

"Come on, you two," her mother called. "Everything's ready."

The evening meal was on the table: potted herrings; tomatoes and lettuce from their little greenhouse; her mother's soda bread and blackcurrant jam. Her father said grace and they began to eat in silence.

"Now tell us all your news," her mother said, brightly, and she handed out their tea.

Leah felt a moment of alarm until she remembered they expected to hear only of everyday experiences such as a child might have. It was Aunt Emily, kind-hearted and understanding, who knew of the real and vital happenings in her life. She had grown secretive with her parents, afraid of their disapproval and of her father's anger over actions considered normal by most people.

So Leah told of shopping with her aunt and of the walks they had taken. "I did weeding in the front garden and helped with the cooking. Aunt Emily loved the dough-nuts I made following Muriel's recipe."

"You went to church, I hope." her father put in. "Though I expect there's too little prayer, too little self-denying in your aunt's place of worship."

Leah stifled a sigh. "Aunt Emily has changed her church. She says it will be nearer for her in the winter. The service is much the same but she likes the extra hymn singing."

Leah's mother said nothing. Her father looked grim. "Typical of Emily - no proper allegiance, either," he said. "I'm very glad you're home again."

Later, in her bedroom, Leah recalled that not so long ago thoughts of church and religion had troubled her greatly. She knew that over the years many people had become dissatisfied with the beliefs and forms of service of the main Protestant churches. They had broken away to form their own little separate groups. Her father's church was one of these small places of worship, each keeping to its own religious doctrines and precepts.

Yet arguments and strife still arose among some of these so-called religious people, and Leah wondered how such diversity of opinion could come from any true Christian faith. There had been times when she had doubted if there really was a God to worship. During her last term at school she had told Muriel about these doubts.

19

Muriel, who usually had an answer to most problems, had said she never thought about it - had just accepted that her own church was right in its teachings.

But soon, in her forthright manner, Muriel had an audience in the school cloakroom when she asked the girls how many really believed in the existence of God.

A few smiled, looked a little surprised and nodded assent. Two or three others gave her a look of disdain and walked away.

"Are you an atheist, Muriel Linton?" one girl called.

"Of course she's not," someone said. "It's right to ask questions." But nobody, it seemed, had anything helpful to say.

Muriel did not give up. One morning, during the final weeks at school, she suddenly raised her hand and put Leah's question to their visiting clergyman.

"Please Sir - how can we believe in the existence of God when we have so many churches all with different beliefs about Christianity and religious practices?"

A shocked intake of breath came from the class. Eyes widened, anxious glances were exchanged. The tall elderly man looked thoughtful for a moment. Then he smiled and everyone relaxed a little.

"The answer is simple," he said. "First of all, let us consider the question of the existence of God. He stretched a hand towards the wide windows and the school grounds and fields beyond.

"There we see some of the wonders of this world: trees, flowers, fruit, birds, animals, and the sky above with its untold mysteries. He turned back to let his gaze range over their watchful faces. "And we must not forget ourselves, must we?" A murmur and smiles went round the class.

"And insects, Sir." A few hands pointed to a tortoiseshell butterfly on a high window pane. Another girl indicated a fly buzzing around.

"Yes," the minister said, "even the tiniest creature is a miracle because it has that amazing attribute called Life. But life has to be sustained and that, too, has been taken care of through the recurring seasons of the year. The work of sun, wind, frost, rain... all have a part to play. Then we have the continuing cycle of day and night, and all the other things necessary to maintain life and to renew it."

He looked around the class, watching them all with interest.

"It should be a challenge to us to treat these gifts with reverence and gratitude. Don't you agree, girls?"

Quickly they nodded or spoke their agreement, impressed, yet still waiting expectantly.

"I suppose you are wondering what all this has to do with religion and Christianity and our many different churches? Well, I believe that true religion comes from the heart and mind recognising this miracle of life and holding it in reverence for the Great Creator we call God, who sent His son to guide and help us. I cannot believe that such an amazing world could come about by chance. And we have here one of the most beautiful and fertile countries of the world."

Leah and the class had continued to listen with great interest as the minister went on: "And if some people wish to choose their own form of worship and thankfulness for their lives on earth, or to seek God's guidance in their own way, I see nothing wrong with that - when it is done in all veneration and sincerity.

There are other people," he said, "who forget that God, the Creator, also gave us the ten commandments. When these commandments are broken, distress, suffering and cruelty can follow. Only by keeping to the ways of God can we help to spread true Christianity - no matter what church we attend. "

After that talk in school, any doubts Leah had about the existence of the Great Creator had been dispelled. She saw divine purpose in all life and a choice of doing good or evil. For there was wickedness in the world, too, and Leah believed it came about when people failed to keep God's commandments.

Wrong doings and disturbing happenings were never discussed in her home, newspapers were rarely seen, but Muriel, who was never reticent about anything, kept Leah well informed on all matters.

For the past few minutes, Leah had been standing at the bedroom window looking out on the back garden, weed-free as always, at the neat hedges and rows of plants.

Now, while she emptied her case and tidied her things, her thoughts were again on her own immediate problem. And when it seemed that her father had returned to his Bible reading, she joined her mother in the kitchen. It saddened her that she might have to be

21

a little less than honest to get her own way and made her wonder if God might punish her.

"Mother," she said, "I've had two invitations for this Friday."

Her mother, about to put away some plates, paused, all attention. "Two?" she said, in surprise.

"Yes - one is from the country for a sort of good-bye party for Muriel before she leaves home. I'm afraid," she added quickly, "I haven't been able to tell her yet that it might not be - well, always convenient for me to visit them in future." She hurried on. "Then, as I was passing Helen's, she asked me to her sister's birthday party. So - what am I to say?"

Leah held her breath, waiting. Her mother remained thoughtful for a few moments. "Well," she said, "we'll have to see what your father says. You go on to bed, dear."

When Leah was told she could make one further visit to the country, her heart seemed to expand with relief and delight.

"We'd like you home as soon as possible," her mother added. "And tell Muriel it would be simpler for her to see you here in future."

"Am I never to visit Muriel again? Won't she think it very strange?" Leah was surprised at the unsteadiness of her voice.

"Your lives are changing. You and Muriel will soon have different interests and responsibilities," her mother answered. "Anyway, we'll see by next summer how the friendship has lasted."

Leah sighed. Of course, Muriel would come. But was this to be the end of that other friendship that so often filled her thoughts?

THREE

From Tuesday to Friday seemed an age to Leah. Soon she had made all possible preparations for starting at her commercial college; she had put the finishing touches to two new blouses and a skirt; she had brushed and cleaned her blazer. Finally, she persuaded her parents to let her go to town for further books and pencils.

Her purchases were small but it was wonderful walking around for a time and gazing into shop windows.

She was sitting dreaming on the bus waiting for it to start on the return journey when Helen's brother, Damien, sat down beside her. He was a slightly built young man of medium height with a very pleasant smile and he had obviously made the most of the sun while away camping for two weeks.

"Haven't seen you for a long time, Leah," he said. "Where have you been hiding all summer?"

She blushed, for his words, quite innocent she felt sure, made her feel guilty about having avoided his family for so long.

"And now," he went on, "I hear you're off again and we won't be seeing you at Judith's party."

"I think I'll be going to the country. I'm sorry," Leah said, quietly.

As they drew nearer home, Leah's pleasure at seeing Damien was soon replaced by an anxious feeling that her father might notice them together and show anger again.

To her relief, Damien left the bus early on to call with friends.

"I hope we'll see you soon," he said.

At last Friday came and Muriel arrived in Jim's grey Morris Minor to take Leah to the country - perhaps for the last time. But now she was too excited to worry much about the future. In their light, summer dresses, they waved goodbye to Leah's mother. Soon they were out of the city traffic and flying along. The sun was shining and everywhere looked fresh and colourful after a recent shower.

"This is wonderful," Leah said, gazing around and noting all the changes that had taken place since her previous visit some weeks earlier. To either side lay fields of stubble with stooks of grain beside golden crops still to be cut. The car flashed past lined-up cocks of hay, neatly stacked bales. On hilly grasslands and in the meadows sheep and cattle grazed in lazy content. Orchard trees hung heavy with ripening fruit.

Muriel gave her a quick smile. "I think you're a country girl at heart, Leah. I just wish you were coming with me to do a course at the agricultural college."

Leah sighed. "If only I could. I'm sure you're getting excited."

"Yes and no," Muriel sounded serious. "You see, the family hope I'll forget about Tom when I'm away. It isn't that they don't like him - it's his mother. She's so strict and bossy, Tom has little freedom about the place. They think I'd be unhappy having to live with her. And Tom says his parents would have a fit if they knew we were thinking of getting married in about a year's time.

He's going to buy a second-hand motor-bike and come to see me. He has his eye on a two-fifty B.S.A. that's for sale in the village. Anyway, I want to forget about all this for the moment. Tonight should be great fun, Leah."

As Muriel drove on towards the little village of Muldare, she told Leah all the local gossip since her last visit. She mentioned Ray and her brother Jim helping each other with the harvest. Muriel's home lay on the outskirts of the village and soon Leah could see the church tower high above the surrounding fields, and the rising line of roof-tops in the main street. They were almost there.

She held her breath and took a quick look up to the right towards the grey house with fresh white window frames where Ray Anderson lived. She saw farm buildings, beech trees, an orchard and garden, and down nearer the road on the village side, an attractive bungalow in rustic brick, where Mr and Mrs Sloan lived, two retired teachers from the city.

Then they were over the bridge that crossed the river and, seconds later, Muriel turned in to the left towards the yellow, two-

24

storied house that stood between a large red hayshed and a line of outhouses backed by an orchard.

Arriving at Muriel's had always brought great happiness to Leah. Today, she stared ahead with a sudden ache and a feeling of emptiness. It seemed quite unbelievable that she would not be returning for her usual visits. And somehow, she must now break this news to Muriel.

"You're very quiet, Leah," Muriel remarked as she negotiated the short, stony lane-way that led up to the house between hawthorn hedges and the occasional tree.

"I was just thinking that this could be my last visit - at least for a very long time."

Muriel flashed her a look of surprise. But her face cleared quickly.

"Nonsense," she said. "I intend to be home for all the holidays, never fear. And, of course, you'll be coming here just as usual, I hope."

Leah shook her head. "I wish it were as simple as that. My parents have decided that, in future, you could call to see me."

The car turned sharply and they drew up in the farmyard. "We'll have to see about that," Muriel said grimly. Then she smiled, blue eyes alert.

"Don't worry, Leah. I'll get you back here somehow. Just leave this to me."

Muriel's mother, busy near a back window, smiled out at Leah and held up hands covered with flour. She was a small, stoutish woman, brown-haired and pleasant-looking with the same healthy complexion as her daughter.

Across the yard, Mr Linton and Jim turned to wave as they manoeuvred their herd of cows back to the field after milking. Leah could recognise the various breeds - mostly Shorthorn and Jersey and Muriel's own little black Kerry cow. She had managed once or twice to milk a pint from this docile animal while Muriel had filled a bucket with no effort from a pedigree Shorthorn. Just lately, since the last agricultural show in the city, Jim had been pressing his father to install one of the new milking machines.

As they entered the house, Mrs Linton called a welcome to Leah from the pantry and asked them to check the oven. She was rolling out pastry to cover a large enamel plate piled high with sliced

25

apples from the early windfalls, all sprinkled with brown sugar and cloves.

In the kitchen, a gently purring Aga stove gave out warm, appetising smells as Muriel removed a batch of lightly browned scones.

"Mm - lovely," Leah remarked, and felt again a pang of sadness.

Muriel threw a grandiose gesture towards earlier cooking arranged on trays on the kitchen table. "See - angel cakes, currant squares, rock cakes - all for tonight and made by me!"

Leah dismissed a small stab of envy as she acknowledged this display and helped to pack them into tins. Her own cooking experience at home was more frugal; her mother, from necessity, had to keep the house-keeping to a tight budget.

In Muriel's bedroom at the back of the house, Leah stood at the window attracted by the gently sloping fields with grazing cattle, harvested crops and a few roaming hens and ducks. In spring time she and Muriel had wandered out there along sheltered banks picking long-stemmed primroses and inhaling their cool, fresh fragrance. On the higher ground, up near the village, the small oak wood behind the church had been carpeted with bluebells, violets and anemones and she had stood entranced by the beauty of it all.

Later in the year, the hedges had been draped with pink and white dog-roses and honeysuckle and along the roadsides and bye-ways a profusion of meadow-sweet had helped to fill the air with summer scents.

As Leah remembered those happy days, her gaze kept coming back to rest on the curving river, a field or two away below the house. It was partly hidden by over-hanging branches of alder, hazel and willow and spanned by a wooden-bridge. This was the way that Ray often came - as a shortcut to reach the village and to call with the Linton family - from his own fields on the other side of the river, both there and across the road.

It was out there she had first met Ray during one of her earliest visits. She had offered to take refreshments to the workers in a field because Muriel had hurt her ankle.

"If the lads are too much for you," Mrs Linton had said with a smile, "just leave these things and let them manage for themselves."

As Leah had pondered on these words, she remembered hearing

the throb of a tractor somewhere near and soon the smell of engine oil had mingled with the scent of new-mown hay. No sooner had she entered the field, than she was startled by repeated wolf-whistles from three or four young lads each holding a rake or a pitch-fork and gazing cheekily in her direction. This was something quite new in her experience and she had stopped in embarrassment wondering what to do.

It had been Ray, she learned later, who had hurried forward to take the can of tea and basket of food. "I'll look after these now if you like," he had said with an amused smile. She had thanked him and escaped.

Ray, she discovered later, was always ready to help anyone or anything in trouble, from trying to mend someone's broken-down car to taking out a thorn from a dog's paw.

And now the sight of the river brought other memories. To Mr Linton and Jim out with their guns, the big willow tree beside the bridge was just the old 'sally' tree to which pigeons came to roost after feeding in the corn fields.

"It's a necessary killing," Leah had been told as she stared in distress at her first sight of dead pigeons. "They eat too much of the grain."

"You could help me get them ready for the pot," Muriel had suggested.

And Leah, steeling her feelings and forcing herself to strip the stiff little bodies, had found the feathers came off nearly with the ease of thistle-down. Muriel showed her how to clean out and wash the birds before putting them on to simmer in a little water. Later on, Leah had even enjoyed eating cold, sliced pigeon with salad.

Sadly, she now thought of the coming autumn and winter months when she would probably have no part in the life of this country district.

Would she ever be back, ever see Ray and her friends again?

"What's so exciting out there?" Muriel asked, as she rejoined her. "You should be getting ready for later on."

For some time Leah had wanted to confide in Muriel regarding her feelings for Ray. But there was little to say about a friendship so fragile and uncertain. It would seem presumptuous on her part to think that Ray's kindness and attention meant anything special. Even his letter had been written at Mrs Linton's request.

"We're expecting a good crowd at the hall tonight," Muriel went on as she opened the wardrobe and brought out her new dress. It was all green and white water-lilies in a satiny material, sleeveless, with a broad shiny green belt, and had been bought in the local town.

"It's lovely," Leah said, holding out the wide skirt. Her own clothes were made mostly by her mother who was a splendid dress-maker. The hum of her pedal sewing machine was heard very often through the house.

"Better hang your dress up, too," Muriel advised.

Leah opened her case and shook out her only party dress with its gathered skirt and puff sleeves. The soft material had a tiny floral pattern in pink, blue and green. It had been made for the last school play, ' The Mikado '. Of course, her father had not allowed her to take part in any of the action, but she had joined in some of the singing.

She had thought her dress quite attractive with its blue collar and sash - until she saw the sophisticated model Muriel had produced.

"Your own dress is very pretty," Muriel said, as though reading her thoughts.

Leah smiled. "Yes - for Little Bo-Peep." But she felt no envy of Muriel as she pushed away the blue knitted bolero her mother had made her pack to wear with it.

"Now you enjoy yourself tonight," Muriel advised. "Forget what your parents have said about not coming back here. I'll have a talk with them when I leave you home."

"Oh, no - please Muriel, not yet. It wouldn't do any good. You just don't know my father."

Downstairs again, Leah helped to prepare the evening meal of fried eggs, bacon, tomatoes and potato bread. The sizzling pan with its warm, savoury smells made her hungry. She could have been so happy only for the shadow hanging over her. It seemed most unlikely that Muriel or anyone else could ever change her parents' decision.

"What's keeping those men?" Muriel asked, a little impatiently as she stared through the window into the yard.

"You and Leah could make a start," her mother advised.

"A good idea," Muriel said. "Come on, Leah."

They had finished their meal and were clearing the dishes when they heard Jim and his father enter the house.

"Sorry we're late," Mr Linton said, coming in from washing his hands.

"We have a heifer about to calve and there were other things to be seen to." He gave Leah a warm smile. "And how's my second daughter - all ready for the fun tonight?" His large weathered hand smoothed the few grey strands across the top of his head. Then he rolled down and buttoned his shirtsleeves before taking his seat at the top of the table. He was a big, jovial-looking man whose bright blue eyes could sometimes flash anger, especially, Leah knew, when his son neglected his duties for frivolous past-times.

At that moment, Leah caught a glimpse of Jim rapidly combing his unruly brown locks before appearing. "Great to see you, Leah," he called, hurrying in.

"It should be a grand night when we all get going. I'm afraid I'll be a bit late, though - it'll take a while to get cleaned up after everything." He spread out his hands with a distasteful look at his working clothes.

"And we won't know him when we do see him," Muriel teased, moving quickly towards the hallway. "New jacket, new shirt, new flannels and plenty of hair-cream."

"You watch out," Jim shouted, "or I won't call for Tom." He turned back, grinning, and said quietly: "You'll keep me a few dances, won't you, Leah?"

"I might," she said, with a forced brightness, as she followed Muriel from the room. Jim, who for so long had noticed her only as his sister's school-friend, had surprised her lately with extra attention and whispered comments. And Muriel, she had noticed, seemed to encourage him. Well, very soon, it would no longer matter.

Upstairs again, Leah found Muriel unusually serious. "I was thinking of Tom," she said. "He works so hard from morning to night - for so little return. Those parents of his never want him to go out anywhere. They resent Jim calling for him - certainly his mother does. As for his getting married, she might consider it when he's over forty." Muriel stared towards the window with a determined look. "Well, Tom and I intend to make our own plans. We'll manage somehow. When I finish my course, I hope to start a proper poultry business. Ray's sister, Louise, told me about her

29

cousins, Lucy and Frances, who are making a great go with their egg-business, keeping deep-litter hens."

Muriel seemed to notice Leah's lack of response at the mention of Ray's family. "Sure you know Ray's cousins, Leah. You've seen the younger girl at the hall, you've danced with their brother, Johnny - and you must have seen Louise at some of the village functions."

Yes, Leah had observed Ray's sister, Louise, with interest. She was a pleasant-looking, dark-haired girl, very quiet and a little older than Ray. They both lived with their mother. Only three years ago their father had been killed in a car accident while driving on an icy road. Louise, travelling with him, had been badly hurt and was still a little lame.

Ray had had to leave the University after just starting his second year, to take over the running of the farm. Leah knew he often came to ask Mr Linton's advice about problems with cattle and crops. He was like one of the family.

"Yes, I know Louise," Leah said. "She keeps lots of hens, too, doesn't she?"

"You couldn't miss all her rows of hen houses up the field beside their orchard," Muriel stated. "She keeps Rhode-Island-Reds and Leghorns mostly. And she always has a great flock of turkeys for Christmas. Do you know she gathers nettles and chops them into their food - says it keeps them healthy? She's a very hard-working girl and a great help to Ray."

Muriel seated herself at the mirror. "It's time I got my war-paint on," she announced. "Sure you wouldn't like to touch up?"

Leah shook her head, saying it would be better for her to return home with no further sins on her conscience.

When Muriel had thoroughly creamed her face, she flapped on a heavy dusting of pink, scented powder with a large swan's-down puff.

"I thought this might help to tone down my rosy, outdoor complexion." She regarded her efforts with some amusement, then lifted a comb and put it into swift action through her mid-brown hair that hung straight past her ears and then turned outwards helped by plastic curlers she had worn the previous night.

She flashed Leah a daring grin. "You don't know how lucky you are, Leah, with your honey-coloured, ready-made curls, innocent cornflower-blue eyes and a sylph-like figure! So, cheer up! I'm sure you're far from finished with us, yet. Come on - now for the glad rags and then we'll be off."

FOUR

As they left the house, Leah felt nervously excited. She was also conscious of a deep sadness as they passed the shadowy trees, heard the call of a bird, the lowing of cattle. With jackets over their finery, and avoiding rough patches on the path, they turned on to the road as it swept round in a rising curve towards the hall on the outskirts of the village. It was here the Y.F.C. held their meetings and social evenings.

Soon they could hear the steady beat of a vigorous Irish reel. On a stream of light the lively notes came tumbling out to meet them with increasing volume and welcome. Leah loved this old-time dance music. Sometimes she had heard Jim, Ray and Tom playing similar tunes on mouthorgans in the Lintons' barn when rain had chased them from the fields.

"Wouldn't you know the Nesbitt brothers all right - with their fiddle and accordion," Muriel remarked. "They can play any tune you ask for. Some of the lads about here want jiving sessions this winter. Of course, it's our Jim who's keenest to get started. He says jiving has taken over in a big way in some of the city dance-halls. Lindy Cummings from the village told him.

"Just in time, ladies." A group of grinning young farmers inside the door moved aside to let them enter. Welcoming words and smiles came from around the hall where many girls were seated, all dressed up and bright-eyed in an atmosphere lightly perfumed.

"Take your partners for the Lancers," someone called, and there was a rush of young men from various directions claiming the girls. Leah felt a moment of panic as Muriel was whisked away.

Then someone spoke her name and her heart did a somersault. There was only time to exchange smiles as Ray guided her quickly to a group of dancers. Soon they were all moving in line forwards and back, meeting and leaving. Partners were changed and often Leah found herself whirled off her feet to the exuberance of the music.

When Ray reclaimed her at one stage she was breathless. He laughed and swung her round again. "Our band's in great form tonight," he said, "with the Glencoe Reel." And his excitement seemed to match her own; her heartbeat quickened. Soon she would thank him for his letter.

"I'm glad you were able to come tonight," Ray said as the dance ended. "Otherwise I'm sure Muriel would have been most disappointed." And now his voice sounded strangely formal, deflating Leah's happiness.

"Thank you for letting me know," she said quickly, looking away. It came to her now that perhaps Muriel had asked Ray, as a family friend, to help them give her a good time on her short visits among them; perhaps that was his only interest in her.

Then, as he left her back to Muriel, he suddenly bent towards her and whispered: "Keep me the next waltz - please, Leah."

Everything was wonderful again. She held her breath and nodded.

Muriel was indicating the arrival of Jim and Tom, both looking well-scrubbed and healthy as they carried in the cake boxes to join the array of food in the adjoining kitchen. When Jim reappeared in his new tan dog's tooth sports-coat and grey flannels, he asked Leah for the next dance, a quick-step. Soon she was trying to match his expert manoeuvring round the crowded floor.

"You're turning into a right wee dancer, Leah. Don't forget I helped to teach you. And soon I hope to get you at the jiving!" Jim's words only reminded Leah that soon her dancing days would be over. She smiled but made no reply.

She had scarcely sat down when she heard the beat of 'The Merry Widow' waltz and Ray was beside her. As they moved off, he said softly: "My favourite dance - especially with you, Leah."

"I like waltzing, too," she said, her heart racing, and not only because they spun around, reversed and spun again.

A slow fox-trot with a neighbouring young man was followed by a 'Paul Jones' with a few unknown partners. Then, as she circled the room again with Ray in a quick step to the tune 'You Are My Sunshine . . .', they saw Jim with Lindy Cummings whose parents kept the village post-office. They were trying some strange, dancing steps in a corner of the hall.

Ray looked amused. "Jim won't be happy until he has everyone jiving, and I must say that young lady has brought him on well."

Muriel had told Leah that Lindy often went dancing in the city when she stayed with friends. She was a pretty girl, very friendly. Tonight, she was wearing a yellow, flared skirt and black top and her straight, blonde hair was tied in a pony tail with a large black bow. She was moving very quickly in gold-coloured high-heeled shoes.

The music had suddenly changed to what someone said was a Rock 'n' Roll number and dancers had stopped to watch. Jim, holding Lindy's hand, swung her round, skirt and hair flying. Then they faced each other, coming together, breaking away and swinging again. A few other couples were beginning to try out the steps with much laughing.

Shortly after this, while Leah was dancing with Jim in a military two-step, he urged her to have a go at jiving at the next opportunity.

"Oh, no - I couldn't" she insisted.

"Oh, yes, you could; you're a natural dancer. Please, Leah." He gave her one of his little-boy, persuasive smiles. "You see, Leah, I have a special reason for asking."

"No, Jim - it's impossible. Please don't ask me."

"All right," he said, as the music stopped. "We'll have a go at home tomorrow with a Bill Haley record. I'll get Muriel to tell you what I have in mind." He squeezed her hand and was gone.

During supper, the hall rang with laughter and chatter. Trays of tea, sandwiches and cakes were handed round several times. The younger people crowded round Muriel to question her about the course on poultry-keeping she was about to start, and to wish her well.

When everything was cleared away, a young man was called on to give them a song. He sang, 'When Irish Eyes Are Smiling', and others joined in the chorus. Two girls followed with a Ruby Murray favourite, 'Softly, Softly'. A friend of Jim's, smiling over at Muriel, began the song, 'Wish Me Luck As You Wave Me Goodbye', and everyone joined in. Leah felt an ache around her heart; the words could be for her, too.

Before the night was over, Leah had danced with many partners and finally with Ray again. He spoke now of Muriel's early departure and of how she would be missed in the district, not only for herself, but for the way she organised meetings and gatherings as secretary of the Young Farmers' Club.

He then asked about Leah's own plans for the future and she told him of the secretarial course she hoped to take. As they stood together for a few moments in the noise and movement of people departing, she wanted to tell him she would not be back for her usual visits. But again, he was in one of his thoughtful moods.

She turned away, looking around for Muriel, feeling there was something strangely withdrawn about Ray's behaviour towards her at times. He was not always at ease with her; sometimes she caught a look of strain in his eyes and wondered if there was someone, somewhere else, he would rather be with. But he was trying to be kind to her - it seemed the only possible explanation. Well, after tonight, it would not matter any more.

When Leah left the hall with Muriel and Tom, the whole countryside seemed touched with magic. A brilliant glow, patterned with strange shadows, lay over houses, trees, fields. The curving road before them was like a silvered ribbon. At home, her favourite view of the full moon was when it appeared as a shining sphere in a deep-blue vaulted ceiling over their garden, flood-lighting the rooftops as she watched from her bed.

But here, tonight, she could feast her eyes in all directions on this scene that she loved. As she marvelled anew at the amazing power of the Creator, she silently sent up a prayer of wonder and thanksgiving and asked that she might be allowed to come back quite soon.

A sudden rustling in the hedge startled her and Muriel laughed. "You're a nervous one, Leah. That was probably a poor bird disturbed from its sleep - or only a twig falling."

Just then hurrying footsteps sounded from behind them and Ray moved in beside her. As she held her breath, she heard him say: "I was hoping to have a word with Jim about some calves he's selling, but he has driven off with Lindy and a couple of others he's taking home. So I'll see him in the morning."

"I'll bet he and Lindy are tired after all that swinging carry-on," Tom remarked. Soon they were discussing the events of the night and all agreed it had been a most enjoyable time.

"We must do this again before Christmas," Muriel declared. "When I get back, of course!" She flashed Leah a look to include her in their plans.

As they approached the house, Muriel and Tom slowed down to lean against the wall at the road. Leah and Ray moved on to the gateway where they stood a little awkwardly some distance apart.

"You'll come, too, for the next night at the hall, won't you, Leah?" And now Ray looked tense and anxious. But even as she wondered, she knew it could be the play of shadows on his face cast by the moonlight through the trees.

"I'm not very sure," she said, and turned aside to lean her arm on the gate. How could she possibly explain what her parents had decided for her?"

He reached out and took her other hand. "You're cold," he said, and enclosed her fingers in his. "Please, Leah - you must come. Say that you'll try to make it."

The sudden warmth and strength of his hand, the entreaty in his voice and her own hopeless position made her want to cry.

"I don't think I'll be back," she said, with difficulty. "Not for a long time, anyway." Her words sounded stiff and uninterested: Yet it seemed her heart was breaking.

"I see," he said quietly. "We'll miss you, Leah!" He released her hand and moved away. Out on the road, he called to the others: "I'll have a word with Jim, tomorrow. Goodnight all." She heard his footsteps fading like her dreams into the distance.

Muriel joined her and Tom turned towards the village. "If I'm lucky," he said, "I might meet Jim coming back and maybe he'd run me home." He waved and was gone.

"Listen," Muriel whispered as she and Leah hurried towards the house, I've a wonderful idea for getting you back here as usual. It's a bit complicated so I'll tell you the plan when we're ready for bed."

Leah sighed. Muriel did not realise how firm her parents could be.

"I thought Ray went off very quickly," Muriel remarked as they quietly undressed. "I always feel so sorry for him - his whole life upset by that tragic accident. He's in a worse position than Tom. He has his mother and sister to care for on top of all other responsibilities. And there's an older brother and two other sisters away from home." She stopped suddenly, her eyes on Leah. Then she went on: "Dear knows when poor Ray can think of getting married. Not that he seems keen on anyone. He danced mostly with his two cousins and you tonight. There's no special girl-friend that I've heard of. That lovely bungalow below their house, that has been let to the Sloans, was built for his parents to retire to - when the time came."

Leah could find nothing to say. She quickly folded her clothes and sank down at the bedside to pray for guidance and help. After a few minutes, she slipped into the big double bed, wishing she could lie down and try to forget everything.

But Muriel bounced in beside her. "Now for my great plan," she announced. "And don't you dismiss it before I get started. I never told you, but this is something I've always hoped for - and now my idea has had a great boost from Jim." She turned to Leah in some excitement. "Of course, I've seen it coming."

Leah waited, not very hopeful that anybody could do anything to help her.

"Well," Muriel said, smiling and throwing Leah a knowing look. "Jim danced with you a lot tonight, didn't he? You must be aware that he's been taking great notice of you for some time now. He's very fond of you, Leah. As I left the hall he told me he would like to take you tomorrow night to one of the big dance-halls in the city. He says you learn fast and jiving would be no trouble to you - with a bit of practice tomorrow. You can easily stay on till Sunday - we'll phone your neighbours, the Fergusons, and they'll tell your parents. You *will* go with him, won't you, Leah?"

Leah had been looking at her in dismay, trying to stop her. "Muriel I couldn't, I couldn't. You should know it's impossible. Jim can take Lindy - she's the expert." Leah wondered what Muriel was thinking of; this was no solution to her problem; it could only implicate her in further lies and deceit. Besides, she would never consider going dancing with Jim.

"Lindy's good fun," Muriel said. "But the family don't really approve of her. They think she's too flighty. But they wouldn't object to him taking you."

"You know I couldn't go," Leah repeated. Surely Muriel could understand that. Her voice rose as she added firmly: "And I don't want to go."

Muriel looked surprised. "But you like Jim, don't you?"

"Yes - of course I like him."

"And I thought you liked dancing with him?"

"Yes - but I like dancing with others, too." Leah held her breath for a moment and then added quickly: "especially with Ray."

But Muriel had not even noticed. She went on, her voice a little impatient "I'm not just talking of dancing, Leah. That's only to get you and Jim to know each other better. You see, my whole plan depends on the two of you falling for each other - like. Tom and me. And Jim likes you, immensely. Please give him a chance, Leah. Don't you see - then your parents would have to think again about stopping you coming here."

Muriel turned to her, eyes widely smiling. "Wouldn't it be wonderful! We might even have a double wedding in the family!"

"Muriel - stop this, please. You don't understand." Leah studied the pink eiderdown for a second. Then she looked up. "There's something I've been wanting to tell you. I've nothing against Jim. It's just that - well, I think I've fallen for Ray."

"Ray Anderson! Oh, Leah, no! Well, you've got to forget about him, and quickly. Ray is a Roman Catholic - with a brother at a seminary and two sisters training to be nuns! Your parents would go out of their minds."

Leah's heart had dropped like a stone. A coldness came over her face. Her voice came out a whispered cry: "Muriel - why did you never tell me?"

"Leah, Leah how could I? I was afraid you'd never come back. Look how your parents stopped you seeing Helen's family. Besides, we never think about Ray's religion; he's one of our best friends. We like Louise, too. The other members of his family are older and they've been away so long we scarcely know them."

Leah felt numb with shock and the thought of her parents' anger frightened her. She sat staring before her with nothing to say.

Muriel's face brightened. "Look, Leah - you haven't seen that much of Ray to be taking this notion of yours seriously. Sure we all like Ray. And when the time comes, he'll choose a nice girl from his own church."

Leah turned away and lay down. She stared at the flowered wall-paper trying to still the thudding of her heart and telling herself that this news made it so much easier for her to go away and never return.

Muriel said, quietly: "Leah, I'm sorry, truly sorry. But you're such a quiet one, I never thought of anything like this happening. I was just hoping that in time it might be you and Jim - and just lately it seemed to be going that way."

She lowered her voice to its most persuasive. "Why not give Jim a chance, Leah? Go dancing with him tomorrow night. It would take your mind off other things. And just think - married to Jim you'd be living here always, in this house. Oh, Leah, it would be perfect! You know you love the country life. And Tom and I would be only a few fields away."

Leah lay quite still, her thoughts in turmoil. Muriel's plans were of no interest to her. That was all she knew.

"All right," Muriel said. "It's not fair to bother you now; you need time to think things over. We'll talk about this tomorrow."

Leah lay awake for a very long time, and not only from a sense of despair. It seemed to her now that perhaps this problem about religion explained Ray's uncertain behaviour towards her. His own family would not welcome any serious friendship between them. Well, it wasn't likely to happen. She was going away now, never to return.

She told Muriel in the morning and asked to be taken home as soon as possible while Mr Linton and Jim were working away from the house. Mrs Linton showed surprise at her sudden departure, but accepted the fact that she was expected home early. She quickly packed some eggs for Leah to take with her. "Come back soon, dear," she said.

On the journey, even Muriel had little to say. Leah knew they were both stunned by the recent revelations. They were also thinking of the changes that were coming in both their lives.

"I can't believe you won't be back," Muriel kept repeating. "It's just ridiculous."

"You'll come and see me when you get holidays, I hope," Leah said.

"Of course," Muriel assured her. "And next time we meet, I bet you'll have got over this notion of Ray completely. It's just a schoolgirl crush, Leah. You'll laugh about it later on. And when you give me the word, I'll get round your parents to let you come back, at least occasionally, to see us."

But Leah felt it would be wrong to even hope that this could ever happen.

FIVE

In the weeks that followed, Leah found it difficult not to think of Ray. Muriel had advised her to try to forget him completely and, in time, perhaps she might give some thought to Jim. But Leah knew that Jim was just a shadow in her mind compared with Ray - and always would be.

Both were good-looking, pleasant young men, quite tall and strongly built. Jim, with his ready joke and rather cheeky grin was very popular with the local girls. Ray was equally well-liked. But there was something different about him, not only in appearance - very dark wavy hair, sensitive features and mysterious brown eyes - for he had an added dignity, a standing apart that appealed to Leah in her own loneliness. This was not, she felt, due altogether to an awareness of his different religious background among a largely Protestant community; it was a part of his nature.

She had been attracted to Ray because of the person he had always seemed to her to be: quietly friendly, kind and so very trustworthy. Often, she found herself reliving all those precious moments she had spent with him, recalling things he had said, sometimes with that strangely anxious look that had once puzzled her so much or with his sudden smile that had caught at her heart.

More than anything, she remembered their last moments together, the gentle pressure of his hand on hers, his appeal to her - and then his hurried departure. Had he really been so disappointed by her reply as they stood together in the moonlight? Probably she would never know.

Leah's attendance at the commercial college helped to fill the days, as she tried to concentrate on her shorthand, typing and English studies. She had longed to train as a teacher like Helen and other girls from her own school. But now she must do her best in the career chosen for her by her parents.

She was pleased to have one of her school friends, Jenny Harrison, taking the same secretarial course. They usually sat together in class and on fine days walked in the nearby park at lunch time. On a few occasions they called at Jenny's home where her parents kept a grocery store. Her young brother had sung for them and his sister of fifteen had played the 'Anniversary Waltz' on the piano, watched by their proud parents. This happy family atmosphere had reminded Leah of Muriel's home and how much she was missing her visits there.

Some evenings, she helped her mother with dress-making or gardening. She played hymn tunes on the harmonium. A few of these: 'Shall We Gather at the River?' and 'The Old Rugged Cross'. . . she had found in a book of music from her mother's early days when she had attended Gospel meetings in the country.

As for the books she was studying so earnestly, her father accepted these as being on her English course and so they must be suitable reading for his daughter. But Leah was enjoying a much wider selection than the novels of Scott, Dickens, Jane Austen . . . and the Golden Treasury of Verse.

Helen, whom she continued to see quite often, if only on the bus, had lent her works of Irish writers like Frank O'Connor, Mary Lavin and Michael McLaverty, as well as stirring verses by Irish and English poets. All these, together with romantic fiction passed on by Muriel, she read avidly and kept safely hidden in her bedroom.

Muriel wrote often from her college - amusing letters about her work and the other students doing Dairying or Agriculture. She said Tom had arrived to see her on his motor-cycle. It had taken nearly two weeks to overhaul the machine to make it road-worthy and had caused much grumbling from his mother about wasting valuable time. He had also spoken to his parents about getting married, and now his mother was going about with very tight lips and a disapproving look. Muriel had been home briefly for the Harvest Thanksgiving and had helped to decorate the church.

"Jim and Ray were asking for you and hope you'll try to make it for the Christmas Social Night in the hall. I had to tell them it was doubtful if you could get away this time. Jim is still crazy about dancing. He has a different partner these days - a wee girl not long left school. Nothing serious, of course. The great Lindy has a job in a city office and rarely comes home now."

Leah eagerly awaited Muriel's letter after the Christmas break and, when it came, it set her dreaming again. Muriel wrote: "Ray never turned up for our social evening; he called here the following day and said one of the cows had been sick and he had to call the vet. But I'm beginning to wonder about him. He seemed quite anxious to talk about *you* - what you were doing these days, where you were studying and when were we going to see you again? I wouldn't be telling you this only I feel sure you've got over that notion you had about Ray. You have never once asked about him. So I told him you had new interests these days and less spare time for visits to the country. I thought he looked really disappointed. I showed him the birthday card you sent me with its picture of snowdrops and he stared at it for ages.

'Nineteen,' he said. 'So you and Leah are now nineteen.' Somehow, I felt really sorry for him. I think he's lonely at times; he and Jim no longer have the same interests. I told him then we'd probably be seeing you later in the year. I certainly hope so. But I know I shouldn't be giving him any encouragement."

To Leah, this news of Ray was like a sad, haunting melody that she wanted to hear again and again. She carried Muriel's letter everywhere with her - although she knew she must be nursing foolish dreams.

Leah came back to reality badly shaken when the results of her latest tests in typing and shorthand showed she had not attained the speeds she had hoped for. Her parents, greatly worried, asked for Aunt Emily's help to buy her a second-hand type-writer. With great determination, she now put in many hours of practice and also typed a long, weekly letter to Muriel.

There was little chance of hearing anything further about Ray until Muriel returned home on holiday. Her next letter said she was looking forward to seeing Leah and her first outing would be to the city. Tom had written to say his parents had come round a little to the idea of his getting married and were actually showing some interest in the proposed poultry business. He hoped they would give some financial help, too.

Muriel arrived to see Leah at the start of the Easter holidays. She was looking healthier and jollier than ever, wearing a royal blue

43

skirt and matching jacket, edged with navy braid - over a bright pink knitted jumper. Her hair, cut shorter, suited her. She even raised a smile from Leah's father as she described the state of Jim's car, a Ford Popular with squealing brakes and an exhaust pipe ready to fall off. She winked at Leah. They both knew the mileage Jim must have covered, not only on farm business but travelling to dances all over the country.

As Muriel chatted on about her course at the college, Leah longed for a talk in private and she soon suggested showing Muriel her books and type-writer in the bedroom.

"Your letters look so professional now," Muriel said, seating herself at the machine and touching keys and attachments as she queried their uses. "I really must get one of these for my future business purposes," she stated grandly.

She turned to Leah with a knowing smile, her voice lowered. "I've been dying to hear if you have met anyone special at the college or anywhere. You never said anything in your letters - I suppose I'll have to drag it out of you!"

Leah shook her head. "There's nothing to tell, really. One rather pimply youth asked me to come dancing at the Plaza ballroom. Can you imagine that!" She glanced towards the sitting room and her parents. "And sometimes I see one or other of Helen's brothers on the bus or in town!"

Muriel raised her eye-brows. "Well, that won't do, either, I'm quite sure. Anyway," she went on, "you never mention Ray now. I knew you'd forget all right. And he hasn't asked about you this time at all. I feel so relieved. I can soon speak to your parents to let you come back for a summer visit."

Leah did not reply to this. Against all commonsense, she felt only a deep disappointment that Ray seemed to have forgotten her.

When Muriel was in the car ready to leave, she gave Leah a daring little smile. "I haven't given up hope yet, you know, for you and Jim. He talks about you often. I know he appears to be a little wild but there's no real harm in him. I'm sure he'll settle down with the right girl. Hurry on the summer!" She waved cheerfully and drove off.

During the month of April there had been some cool, damp weather and Jenny had been absent from classes for a few days with a very bad cold. On the Friday, when the sun came out again,

Leah walked alone in the park admiring the fresh splendour of massed daffodils and tulips in circular beds and bursting cherry blossom on slender branches bordering the paths. Leaves were opening on trees and hedges, birds were singing and some were building nests. A blackbird passed her carrying a single straw; then it disappeared quickly into the bushes.

The amazing renewal of life was at work again. Leah felt the thrill and wonder of it all. Yet she could not banish an inner sadness as she thought of all that was happening around the little village of Muldare. She sighed and took from her pocket Muriel's latest letter, telling of fields being ploughed and crops planted. "Jim has a new Fordson tractor, and I'm dying to get home to see the new batch of chickens from our latest incubators."

Leah remembered helping Muriel the previous year to turn dozens of eggs hatching in incubators, sprinkle them with tepid water and renew the oil in the heating lamps. Later, she had watched in amazement and delight as damp little creatures tapped their way through the shells and tumbled out. In a very short time, they became lively, chirping bundles of yellow fluff, another of life's miracles.

Folding Muriel's letter sideways, Leah re-read the postscript: "Hip, hip hooray! At last all parents have agreed to a springtime wedding next year for Tom and me. Of course, you'll be my chief bridesmaid. Your parents couldn't possibly refuse me that."

The thought of returning to the country for such a big occasion, and probably seeing Ray again, disturbed and even frightened her. But the event was nearly a year away; she would try to put it out of her mind and concentrate on her exams. She wrote a long letter to Muriel trying to match her friend's happy mood and saying she was looking forward to hearing more of her plans at their next meeting.

Several weeks later, Leah left the college one afternoon with her exams almost over and feeling fairly confident that she had not disgraced herself this time. She waved goodbye to Jenny and found her attention drawn to a small green car at the kerb where the driver was getting out. Then, her heart lurched painfully for she saw that it was Ray.

He came towards her, his smile uncertain, and they shook hands formally.

45

"I - was just passing," he said. "Muriel once mentioned the name of your college." He gave the building a nervous glance. "I - I do hope I'm not keeping you?"

Her excitement ebbed a little; he had not come especially to see her, it seemed. "We finished a bit early today," she explained, adjusting the books on her arm and trying to look unconcerned.

"Well - perhaps I could give you a lift somewhere?"

"Oh, no! No thank you," she said quickly. "I sometimes wait in the park until bus time." She suddenly blushed, realising she had spoken quite without thinking.

Ray's face lit up. "Perhaps - I could come, too?"

She paused only for a second. "If you like," she answered, her heart thumping, her voice almost breathless.

With a smile, he took her books and placed them in the car. She watched, wondering if this was all a dream, and thinking how splendid he looked in green tweed jacket and well-pressed flannels, his dark hair gleaming in the sun. Yet she knew he was the same thoughtful Ray who had caught at her heart, the kindly young man who, for her, had become a vital part of the joyous mystery of life.

They set off together, both very nervous and trying to hide their delight in the present situation. In the park, they were soon laughing at the antics of a small sandy terrier chasing a ball across the grass. Before them lay beds of velvety-brown wall-flowers and yellow antirrhinums, enclosed by a border of blue forget-me-nots. Ray confessed to knowing more about the flowers and weeds that grew along the hedge-rows and in the fields. "But at least I recognise forget-me-nots!" He glanced at Leah.

"My sister, Louise, takes care of the garden. You may have seen her about the village. And she never misses the flower shows."

"Yes, I think I know Louise," Leah said. Suddenly, she was reminded of Ray's other sisters away in a convent - of his brother, a priest. She felt a tightness inside her, an invisible wall dividing them. She knew she should not be there with Ray at all. This was madness.

As they walked on, she was conscious of hearing voices and the thud of tennis balls. Ray indicated the seat overlooking the courts and she sat down, her mind in turmoil.

Ray said: "I've missed you, Leah. Any chance that you'll come our way soon again?"

46

Despair gripped her - like a full-stop to these moments of happiness. How could she ever explain? "I'm - not sure," she said. "It depends on what I'll be doing - if I get my exams." But she knew this did not make sense.

He turned to her, smiling. "Well, I could come to see you, if that would be all right?"

She sat staring before her, unable to find an answer.

Encouraged by her silence, he said, eagerly: "Could I see you some Sunday here, perhaps? I'd like us to be friends, Leah."

"No - no! I'm sorry, Ray. My parents -" She got up quickly and he joined her.

"I know," he said. "Your parents would object because I am a Catholic."

She nodded. "Your people would be against our friendship, too."

"Leah - wait, please! Do you want me to stay away, never to see you again?"

"I don't know. I think it would be better." She continued walking quickly and now he was beside her.

"Leah, I can't help being a Catholic, nor can I help wishing you and I could be friends."

"It just isn't possible," she told him, trying to shut out a picture of her father standing over her in anger.

"I understand," Ray said, with some resignation. And Leah guessed he was thinking of his own family too.

When they reached the car, they were both in a subdued mood. Ray handed out her books and, with a sad little smile, wished her good luck in her exams.

"Thank you. I have to go now. Goodbye, Ray."

"Not 'goodbye' I hope, Leah. Let's say - 'Au revoir'. It doesn't sound so final." He was watching her, anxiously.

She raised a hand and smiled. "Au revoir," she said. And Ray did the same. As she turned away, she felt a sudden lifting of her heart, in spite of the futility of their situation.

For the next few weeks, thoughts of Ray and the difficulties separating them rarely left her. She had told him their friendship was impossible. Yet in her heart this statement did not really make sense. They had recognised a special bond between them right from their very first meeting. Their feelings on life in general had seemed to be in accord. Yet they had been reared in totally

47

different religious environments. She had followed her parents' beliefs only in so far as they seemed right for a truly Christian way of life. But her father lacked any understanding or toleration of other people's faiths, especially those of the Roman Catholic church. So, thinking of any future meeting with Ray both thrilled and frightened her.

Leah had been waiting hopefully for her exam results and was greatly relieved to hear she had passed very well. Now she longed to start work. But, while Jenny and others were busy applying for any jobs they fancied, she had to wait until something turned up that met with her parents' approval. Their careful guarding of her from the outside world made her all the more unhappy about keeping things from them.

Muriel was home again, her course finished, and she and Tom were getting down to serious planning for the future. Leah would have liked a few days with Aunt Emily at the coast but she had to wait until her aunt returned from a visit to her daughter, Carol, in England.

On fine days, Leah worked in the garden - weeding, picking sweet-pea and runner-beans for the house and dreaming of other days. She made two summer dresses with some help from her mother and continued her reading. She was not really unhappy; she had an excited feeling of anticipation. Perhaps a job would turn up any day now and she could begin a life of her own.

Then, early one afternoon, Muriel arrived to see them. In her usual light-hearted manner she praised Leah's efforts in the garden, her mother's needlework, her father's fine crop of tomatoes.

"Which reminds me," she said, with a bright, determined look, "I've come to see if Leah could help us with the church fete tomorrow?" She smiled sweetly at Leah's parents and hurried on to tell them of all the jam and cake-making that had gone on in her own home, with the continual care of vegetables and flowers outside.

"I do hope you can spare Leah to give us a hand with all the preparations. She has been a great help to us in the past, you know."

Leah found she was holding her breath, her heart pounding as she waited, not sure at all of the answer she wanted her parents to give. And when it was announced that she could return with

Muriel, she stood utterly dumbfounded. Then, in a whirl of anxious excitement, urged on by Muriel, she hurried to get ready.

SIX

As they drove away, Muriel's eyes held a triumphant look. "You see, it was easy! I told you everything would come all right. So cheer up - there's nothing to worry about."

"Muriel," Leah said, "I have seen Ray again." She then told her of their meeting at the college and how they had parted.

"Well, you're a close one, I must say! Just when I thought it was all over between you two and quite safe to bring you back." Muriel looked worried and she continued to warn Leah of the futility of continuing with such a friendship. "I just hope Ray stays away from the fete tomorrow. But there's not much chance of that if he hears that you have arrived."

Among Muriel's friends and neighbours gathered in the church hall, Leah was soon caught up in the excitement of preparing for the following day. But it did little to ease her anxiety and anticipation regarding a probable meeting with Ray. While she longed for this to happen, she still knew she should not have come.

Back at the house, while final arrangements were being discussed with some of the helpers, Leah strolled through the garden to see Mrs Linton's roses. She found all the bushes neatly labelled: McGredy's Yellow and Madame Butterfly were the most eye-catching but Etoile de Holland, a brilliant red, and Betty Uprichard, carmine and orange, both gave out a heady perfume that delighted her. The sun was strong and flowers were opening rapidly. Tomorrow, many of the blooms would be cut and on display.

As Leah went towards the orchard, she heard the occasional plop of a falling apple. The delicious red Victoria plums were not yet ripe, nor the little sugar and water pears, sweet as honey and brimming with juice, that she remembered from a previous year.

Jim and Ray had brought a basin-full into the house saying they should be eaten at once before they were over-ripe.

It was cool and dark among the fruit trees and the grass was long and damp from an earlier shower. These surroundings seemed to add to Leah's sadness and she moved quickly to a patch of sunlight, and stood there deep in thought. When someone called her name, very softly, the voice made her heart pound - at first joyously but then with something like despair.

Ray was standing at the orchard gate, his eyes focussed on Leah with a look of delighted misbelief. "I felt sure I must be dreaming," he said. "I was thinking of you as I came down the field from the village and, suddenly, there you were - just over the hedge."

In her heart, Leah had willed this meeting to happen, regardless of what the future might hold. But now all her feelings of love and guilt and fear were just a tangle in her mind. She stood speechless and wide-eyed watching him. "Forgive me," Ray said, coming towards her. "I'm sorry - I frightened you. But you looked so beautiful standing there in your flowered dress with the sun on your hair."

"That's called flattery," she put in quickly, trying to hide her nervous delight as he stood beside her smiling and sun-burnt, the sleeves of his faded checked shirt rolled high on muscular arms, his dark hair tossed.

He flicked a few damp strands from his forehead and now his eyes, resting steadily on her, were darkly tense and serious.

"Not flattery, Leah. Never flattery. You must know I'm in love with you. I can think of nothing more wonderful than to be with you for the rest of my life. Could you not give me a little hope, Leah?"

She turned away, her heart pounding. "I can't - you know I can't." Yet what he had said only echoed her own secret hopes.

Gently, he turned her towards him, a hand on her arm. Listen, Leah. You and I belong together. I have believed this for a long time. Other people in similar circumstances to ours have got married. So why can't we?"

She stiffened, remembering the story of her father's sister, told by Aunt Emily, and Muriel's accounts of heart-break among families of mixed-marriage partners whose religious differences had proved to be unsurmountable.

She stood speechless, shaking her head. Then, from the house they heard Muriel calling her. "I'll have to go," she said, looking at him in despair.

"But we *must* talk about this, Leah. You know we must. I'll see you tomorrow at the fete."

She gave him a troubled glance of assent and hurried away.

It was late that evening when Leah told Muriel of her meeting with Ray in the orchard, and of their intention to see each other the following day.

"Oh, Leah, until this afternoon I was so happy about bringing you here again. Now I find you all starry-eyed and excited telling me that Ray has actually mentioned marriage! This is crazy! Think of the differences in the religious backgrounds of your people and Ray's. Your beliefs are so simple and unadorned, I can't see you ever changing."

Leah felt sudden alarm. "Please Muriel, I'm not thinking so far ahead."

"Well, Ray certainly is - from what you tell me. You'd have to turn, you know, and become a Catholic. With a family like his there's no alternative. Think of his brother, a priest, and his other two sisters in the convent. Think of your own parents! Oh, Leah, what are we going to do about you?"

Leah sighed. "It's no use telling me to forget Ray." Then she smiled. "At least, you don't have to start worrying yet; I won't be twenty-one for some time."

Muriel's look softened. "Whatever happens, Leah, just remember I'll be with you all the way. And now I think I ought to tell the family something of this. It's going to be quite a shock for them."

Leah awoke the next morning to sounds from the yard and kitchen; everyone was up and busy. She was amazed she had slept so well. Today, she knew, could possibly be a turning point in her life.

She washed and dressed quickly. Putting on her lilac cotton dress with the white collar and cuffs and her new white sandals made her close her eyes on a wave of guilty feelings. Her mother had helped to make the dress, choose the sandals. Her father had given her an extra ten shilling note of pocket money to spend. Yet, today of all days, such thoughts must be pushed away.

Sunlight was streaming over dew-drenched fields and no clouds marred the blue of the sky as she lingered at the window anxiously considering the coming meeting with Ray before she joined Muriel, downstairs. But no matter how she thought of their problem there seemed no solution.

By afternoon, excitement was high in the field beside the church. Muriel was in charge of the cake stall where a fine array of fruit-cakes, pastries, sponges and biscuits all looked most professional. Nearby, Mrs Linton had spread out her colourful assortment of embroidered tray-cloths, doilies, linen tea-cloths, boxes of handkerchiefs, cushion-covers, including two presented to Muriel by Leah's mother as they were leaving.

Leah looked away as a further feeling of distress washed over her.

Before the opening ceremony, she was able to help Muriel with price tickets and run here and there with messages for other stall-holders. But later, Muriel wished her luck and told her to enjoy her brief holiday while she waited for Ray.

For a time she stood watching the children's races - the Donkey Derby, a sack race . . . She heard their excited squeals. Then she walked round the stalls saying a few nervous words here and there to people who remembered her and welcomed her back. But all the time her thoughts were really elsewhere and she felt in a kind of panic, especially when she glanced through the trees down towards the river and the bridge - the way that Ray would come. Supposing he didn't turn up at all? She couldn't bear to think of that. But Muriel, of course, would say it was all for the best.

Moving on, she was aware of the scent of cut-flowers in water-filled containers, the more earthy smell of neat rows of vegetables. She passed the jams and pickles and stopped at the second-hand book-stall. But soon she realised she was turning pages and staring at words and illustrations without really seeing them.

At the next stall of ornaments and other oddments, she glanced around quickly again, and there was Ray among the crowd, this time very smartly dressed in a cream shirt and grey flannels. He saw her at once and that special smile of his that began in his eyes and spread over his long, sensitive face held her like magic. In that moment, it seemed impossible that they could ever say goodbye - no matter what trouble might threaten them.

"Hello," he said softly, as he stopped beside her. "I came as soon as I could. I suppose you have already seen everything?"

"Not quite," she said, sensing a nervousness in him equal to her own, a consciousness of people watching them. They surveyed the objects on the stall and Ray lifted the delicately carved fruit-bowl that she had been admiring. The surface had a silky smoothness below a band of raised flowers and leaves. She had thought it beautiful but too expensive for her.

"I'd like to buy this for you," Ray whispered. "It's the work of a local craftsman."

"Oh, no - please," she said, hurriedly. How could she ever take home a gift from Ray? She now chose for her mother a colourful butter-dish, brown and yellow, for which she paid three shillings and sixpence. For Mrs Linton she bought a pretty flower-pot with a painted design of green and cream costing five shillings. The potter's name, A. Lowry, was inscribed on the base.

As they turned to go, Muriel reached them. "I've been searching for you two," she said, with a certain look of concern. "I'm free for a cup of tea now. Let's leave your parcels somewhere safe and join the others."

In the refreshment tent, background music was competing with the continual noise and chatter. Leah and Muriel joined Jim and Tom already seated with a plate of ham sandwiches and cream buns. Ray soon arrived carrying a tray with steaming cups and an assortment of pastries. They talked of the great turn-out of people, the array of goods on show and the splendid weather they'd had all week for harvest work. As they all tried to laugh and joke as usual, Leah was conscious of a constraint among them; they were wondering about Ray and herself for Muriel had already prepared them.

And Leah had a sinking feeling as she, too, wondered about their impossible situation.

Soon they saw Jim's glance turning towards the tent entrance. Then he jumped up.

"Someone I have to see - excuse me, all." He winked, and flashed them his usual light-hearted grin.

"Whoever she is," Tom stated, with his slow smile, "she will have to be a smashing dancer - all ready for the coming season!" This gave them all a laugh, knowing Jim.

54

Then the four of them wandered out among the crowd where greetings were exchanged and summer outfits admired by Leah and Muriel. When they paused at Mrs Linton's stall, the two men tried their skill at an adjacent dart-throwing competition. As Leah left Muriel back to her own stall, they passed Ray's sister and two friends who waved to them. And Leah noticed that Louise gave her a long, anxious look.

When she rejoined Ray, Tom was about to return home. "Duty calls," he said. "So long you two - and the best of luck."

Leah and Ray took the path towards the river. Very soon Ray would have to leave, too. They smiled at each other wordlessly as they made their way past running, squealing children playing round the trees. Ray took Leah's hand when she seemed in danger of being knocked down. Then, at the edge of the wood, they stopped.

"I have decided, Leah," Ray said. "There is only one thing to do: I must see your parents and tell them about us."

She looked at him, sadly. "My father would never agree to see you."

"But Leah, how else are we to meet again? You have told me - and I agree - you can't go on deceiving them."

She stared at the ground, moss covered and threaded with massive tree-roots. "I'll tell them myself," she said, suddenly, looking up. "I'll speak to my mother before I go to stay with Aunt Emily - very soon now." Her heart was hammering; it seemed she had set herself the impossible.

"Then write to me - at once," he said. "Perhaps your mother would talk to me? In any case, I'm coming to see you, if I may, when you go to the coast. I like the sound of your Aunt Emily." He smiled, trying to cheer her up.

They set off together, then, down towards the river and back through the trees, talking of their difficulties and trying to see a clear way through the gloom. The sun was going down as they said goodbye. Ray drew her gently towards him and held her for a few moments. "Remember, Leah, I truly love you and it saddens me deeply to bring you this distress. But I feel sure that we'll pull through." He kissed her lightly on the forehead and she had to hold back the tears. Then he left, waving once, and was soon out of sight.

But Leah knew that her trouble was not solely the reaction of her parents to the knowledge of Ray's religion. She also had doubts that she could ever change her own religious life to match Ray's as he must hope she would.

She had tried to tell him this but he had not quite understood.

"We'll work something out, you'll see," he had said, eagerly. And while she felt a surge of happiness at the thought that he loved her and was prepared to face the angry disapproval of both her family and his own, a weight of foreboding lay heavily on her heart.

As she walked back thinking of what she had to tell her parents, Leah felt dazed and frightened in an unreal world. She saw the crowd was thinning, the sun had disappeared. Some of the stalls had nearly sold out; the last of the lemonade and buns were going rapidly at half-price and Muriel was very busy among the stall-holders clearing up. A wave of loneliness and despair gripped her.

When Mrs Linton appeared ready to go home, Leah gladly offered to join her and help carry her load of purchases: cakes, linens, other people's jam and a huge vegetable marrow.

They waved goodbye and set off through the village where Mrs Linton exchanged pleasantries along the way and Leah did her best to smile and show interest.

Out on the empty road, the village left behind, Muriel's mother gave Leah a troubled look. "Leah, dear, we've heard about you and Ray and your fondness for each other. Dear child - you mustn't do anything rash."

"We've known each other for nearly three years," Leah said defensively.

"I know, Leah - and he's a very attractive young man, with the highest of principles and utterly trustworthy. Nobody knows that better than we do. But you must think of your family and of the worry and distress such a friendship would cause them. From what Muriel tells me, it seems unlikely that your father would ever accept Ray as a son-in-law. And just think of the upset there's bound to be in Ray's home."

As Leah said nothing, she went on in a more hopeful tone: "I know it seems hard, dear, but you are both young - you'll get over this in time."

Leah stared ahead, saying nothing, conscious of a tightening pain inside her head, a throbbing at her temples. Again and again, she had prayed for guidance in this matter; she had asked for forgiveness for letting it happen. But, so far, no inner voice had warned her to do as Muriel's mother was advising.

It was a relief to see Mr Linton waiting near the house to hear all the news from the field. But there was a forced gaiety among them as they recounted some of the events. Soon Leah said she would wait at the road for Muriel coming. She wanted so much to have the ordeal with her parents over and done with, to hide nothing further from them, no matter what their reaction might be. And that was something she dared not even think about.

An hour or so later, with rain falling lightly, she and Muriel arrived in the city. They were both subdued and had said little on the journey.

There seemed nothing more to say until Leah had spoken to her parents.

"Please write to me soon, Leah. I'll be so anxious about you."

Muriel stayed for only a few minutes, pleading much clearing up to be done at home. "I felt such a traitor," she said, getting into the car, especially when your mother thanked me so much for having you and for bringing her the box of cakes. She likes your butter-dish, too. And my mother was delighted with the present you bought for her. Oh, Leah, why has it all to be so sad?" She regarded Leah anxiously. "And now I hear your aunt is coming for you tomorrow morning."

Leah nodded. "Yes, and I'm glad. This will make things easier. I'll tell mother about Ray tonight."

"Oh, Leah - I do hope you're doing the right thing." And she waved, "Goodbye and good luck."

For the rest of the evening, Leah was busy getting ready for her holiday with her aunt. She was relieved when her father soon left to take his Bible class. Their neighbour, Mr Ferguson, would drive him home later. Before that happened, she hoped to have told her mother everything and tried to make her understand.

Over and over she rehearsed how she could begin. But the more she thought about it, the more difficult it became. At last, hearing her mother come in from the garden, she approached the kitchen.

"Mother," she said, her voice strangely high, "I've something very important to tell you." She took a deep breath. "You see -

someone from the country - has said he'd like to marry me. Not immediately, of course." Put baldly like that, Leah knew it sounded all wrong.

Her mother turned quickly, eyes startled. Then she relaxed and looked amused. "Some old farmer, I bet, having a joke with you. I know what they're like." She continued drying dishes.

"He's - he's not old," Leah said, trying to control the words and seeing a picture of Ray smiling down at her. "He's a young farmer called Ray Anderson - who was at the village school with Jim and Tom. Muriel's family think very well of him. And he's very serious about this, Mother."

"Leah, Leah, he thinks he is, you mean. He'll get over it, don't worry. Just forget about the whole thing. Anyway, you might never see the young man again."

"Mother - please listen. I can't forget. You see - I like Ray, very much. He - he wanted to come to see you and Father - only, only -" Her voice, trembling so much, refused to go on.

"Leah - stop this nonsense at once! Your father won't welcome any young farmer, I can tell you that. It's not the life we want for you. Besides, what do you know about this young man? You haven't been near the place for a year." Her voice softened. "Look, dear, we won't mention this to your father. It's just a girlish notion, probably encouraged by Muriel, and something we did not want to happen. You go to bed, now. Your aunt hopes to call for you early tomorrow."

Leah felt a moment of panic. But she had made a promise to Ray and the thought gave her renewed strength. "Mother," she burst out, "it's not like that at all. Ray and I are both serious about each other. And Father has got to be told. You see - Ray is a Roman Catholic!"

At the sight of her mother's shocked expression, Leah's face crumpled. But she had to finish. "I have loved him for a very long time. But I did not know about his religion then. He is truly good and kind, Mother. If only you would -"

Her mother was staring at her with a fixed and frightened look.

"Oh, Leah - have you taken leave of your senses? Don't you know this will kill your father?"

Leah turned and fled to her room, her tears now uncontrollable. For hours, it seemed, she lay in the darkness, long after her father's

58

return when the house was quiet again and his angry voice had ceased to reach her. She went over and over every word that had passed between herself and her mother. It had been like a nightmare. Yet there was still worse to come; how could she face her father at breakfast-time? She tossed and turned, her head aching until she finally fell asleep.

It took all her courage that morning to enter the kitchen. Her mother's face looked drawn and miserable as she regarded Leah.

"I'll hope you have come to your senses again," she said, opening a drawer and taking out cutlery, "because if you haven't - I'm afraid your father never wants to see you again." With quick, uncertain movements, she began to butter toast. That finished, she looked up and added, persuasively, "But I know, dear, you won't go on with this madness. After your holiday you'll come back to us our own, sensible girl." She poured Leah a cup of tea, then placed the teapot and some breakfast things on a tray which she lifted and took with her from the room.

Leah knew now that her father did not intend to appear until she had left the house. While she felt a great sense of relief, it also brought home to her the enormity, in his eyes, of her revelation, and the punishment he was prepared to give her.

She was afraid to think of the future as she finished her packing, adding extra clothes and other things she would need. Her legs felt weak and she was trembling.

When her aunt's car arrived in the drive, she hurried out and whispered that it would be better for her not to come into the house. Her mother had now appeared, standing nervously at the door, and Aunt Emily called to her: "Can't wait - I'm on my way to see Jane and the new baby."

As Leah lifted her case from the hall, her mother leaned over and put some holiday money in her pocket. "Remember what I've told you, dear. Have a nice holiday and, when you come back, we need never mention this unfortunate business again."

"Goodbye Mother," Leah said quietly. She felt strangely calm now as she moved away. From the car, she waved and they were off.

"Poor Margaret looks as though she could do with a holiday," her aunt remarked. "And what was all that about not letting me in?"

Leah sighed. "My parents are very upset - all because of me."

She began then to tell her aunt the whole story.

"So now it seems I have no home - unless I agree never to see Ray again. But I can't do that, Aunt Emily. I'll have to find work - anything - as soon as possible."

"Oh Leah, this is terrible ! No wonder your poor mother looks so ill. I do hope you know what you're doing. I suppose this is the young man you told me about last year?"

Leah nodded. "For me he has always been someone special."

"Well, we'll have to talk this over when we get home. But you do see, Leah don't you, that it puts me in a very awkward position with regard to your parents."

SEVEN

Waking up in Aunt Emily's house the following morning gave Leah a momentary sense of pleasure. Then, suddenly, she stiffened, closing her eyes on a wave of anguish at the memory of what had happened the previous day. But hovering in the background was a feeling of relief that at last her parents knew about Ray and she had no longer to deceive them.

She had had a long talk with her aunt on their return from seeing Leah's cousin, Jane, her husband John and baby Adam on their farm thirty miles north of the city.

"Well now, Leah," her aunt had begun, when they were seated at supper, "tell me what is so special about this young man that you are prepared to desert your parents for him and change your whole way of life?"

Leah stared beyond the room, seeing Ray in all his moods: laughing, angry, teasing, thoughtful - and always with a helping hand when needed. But, of course, there was more than that to Ray. For her, there was a magic something about him that touched her heart. And always they seemed to enjoy the same things, even in their choice of music, their reading.

She turned to her aunt. "I don't really know," she said. "We just understand each other so well. Ray means everything to me."

Aunt Emily looked worried. "Apart from other serious considerations, I don't see you as a farmer's wife, Leah."

"That won't happen until I'm over twenty-one," Leah told her.

"Besides, Muriel says the new working methods on the land are beginning to make farming life much easier for everyone concerned."

"I'm glad to hear all of that," her aunt said. "And much can happen in the meantime. Anyway, I feel I should warn you that it's possible you have surrounded this young man with an aura of mystery - even glamour - because of his different background, religious and otherwise. And he may feel attracted to you for similar reasons. This may not last, Leah. You are the girl who soon found your parents' life-style and religion too restricting. And I know you can be just as single-minded as your father on certain matters." She gave Leah a cautionary smile. "But I also know, you will always follow your parents' sound, basic teaching."

Leah interrupted, reminding her aunt that she had not known of Ray's religion until a year ago. "I have always liked and admired him; that's all I know." She looked away quickly, hiding a rush of tears. The events of the past two days were suddenly overwhelming her.

"Oh, Leah - I've upset you," Aunt Emily said. "But I'm only anxious for your happiness. Anyway, we're both tired now. And please, don't worry, dear; I'll help you as far as I can."

When they met at breakfast, Aunt Emily said, cheerfully: "Well, now, what about making a start to find you a job - right here in this small town. We'll have a look at 'situations vacant' as soon as possible."

Leah felt truly grateful that her aunt intended to let her stay at least for the present. Despite the worry about her parents, the days passed quickly as she worked about the house and garden, searched papers for secretarial openings and sent off her applications.

She wrote to Ray for the first time, her heart unsteady, her face flushed with excitement and anxious bewilderment over the action she had taken. Helen and Muriel were told also of all that had happened.

Aunt Emily had been writing, too, and she held out the letter she had ready for Leah's mother:

Dear Margaret,

I want you to know that I intend to stand by Leah no matter what she decides about her future. I find it difficult to believe that you and Matthew would wish me to do otherwise. I have given her problem great thought; Leah has done nothing wrong in the eyes of God - of that I feel sure. I shall, of course, advise her to think very carefully about everything before making any final decisions . . ."

"Thank you, Aunt Emily," Leah said, feeling deeply moved by

her aunt's kindness. Three weeks later, she began her first job in the local office of a building society. She made friends quickly with two very helpful young women, Sadie and Maude, typing beside her in the first-floor room overlooking the sea. It was now into autumn with fewer days of sunshine, but Leah loved the walk home by the sea-front and up the hill to her aunt's bungalow. She liked to dream a little to the accompanying splash of the waves, the smell of sea-weed and the cry of gulls as they swooped low over boats in the harbour. She was happy, too, to be earning her own money and able to contribute something towards her keep. Aunt Emily, however, would accept only a token payment. "You'll soon have to start saving towards that big day you may be contemplating. There won't be any help from parents for you, Leah." Leah knew that only too well. She also had written home, telling about her work and life with Aunt Emily, and how sad she felt about upsetting her parents who had been so good to her. She said she often thought of them and hoped some day they could find it in their hearts to understand and forgive her. But neither Leah nor her aunt received any reply to their letters.

A meeting with Ray had been arranged for the coming Sunday afternoon in the local park. "I thought you might not be very happy if he called for me here at the house," Leah told her aunt.

"My dear girl - how can I help or advise you if I don't know the young man who is causing all the trouble? Of course, you must bring him to see me - even if you don't want my advice."

Sunday brought a morning of sunshine with a near cloudless sky as Leah walked home from church with her aunt. But later, after she had set out for the park in great excitement, grey clouds came drifting by on a sudden breeze. Aunt Emily had waved her goodbye and, with a sad little shake of her head, had told Leah she looked a picture in her new suit.

"It matches those eyes of yours that simply can't hide your happiness."

But now Leah's outfit felt too light and summery, and there was no time to go back. Could this gathering darkness, she wondered, be a warning of coming disappointment? Had Ray's family perhaps convinced him of the folly of continuing with such an unsuitable friendship? The thought filled her with alarm. Yet how happy her parents would be.

When she reached the park her heart was thumping anxiously. Then, suddenly, the sun came out again warm and golden. It came sweeping over the path before her, lighting up the trees, the grass, the flower-beds, chasing the clouds and once more lifting her spirits.

She heard the barking of a dog, children's voices calling. The next moment she saw Ray coming towards her, striding out in his dark, Sunday suit. Soon they were standing smiling at each other in delight and relief that this, their first real meeting, was actually taking place.

"Leah, Leah - I've dreamed of this meeting, many times," he said, clasping her hands as though to make sure she was truly real. Leah, for a few moments, felt too choked with happiness to speak.

They walked on together then, past a line of horse-chestnut trees standing proudly splendid although their leaves were turning brown and yellow, dying and falling. Children had removed the polished brown conkers since Leah's previous visit to the park. Now a hungry looking blackbird, hopping through the grass, eyed them cautiously.

Ray spoke first of the sad break-up between Leah and her parents.

"I can only hope they will come to understand and see us soon."

"Someone like my father never changes his mind," Leah said sadly.

"And are you like your father?" Ray asked, thoughtfully.

"Aunt Emily says I am - in some ways." Then she added more brightly: "Aunt Emily has asked to meet you - to judge if you are a suitable friend for me to have!"

For a moment he looked anxious. "So long as you think I am. Isn't that what really matters?"

"Well - I'll have to see about that - won't I?" Leah kept up her teasing manner and they wandered on.

Resting on a park seat, they were reminded of an earlier meeting and how they had parted so unhappily. Then Leah told about her job and her new friends. And Ray spoke of his farm work - digging potatoes, threshing corn, feeding cattle . . . He mentioned the new buildings going up at the Coulter home in readiness for Tom's marriage to Muriel in the spring.

"And you're to be a bridesmaid, I hear." He smiled. "I hope to be there to see you." He went on to speak of his sisters, Eileen and Kathleen, who would be home for Christmas from the convent.

His brother, Father Stephen, would soon be working on the Missions in South America.

"I can't keep you to myself much longer, Leah. Mother and Louise are asking to meet you. When you and I are married, we'll all be together at the home place - for a time, anyway."

Leah's heart began to race. It seemed that Ray had little doubt about their future together. "I - haven't thought so far ahead," she told him. "After all, we might change our minds!" She tried to smile away her sense of unease.

"Leah - please don't say that. And I can't bear to see you worried. You'll get used to us all very quickly. I feel sure you will."

But Leah wondered how Ray's mother would regard her joining their family. And then there was her own problem. Muriel and her aunt had warned her that, in a family like Ray's, she would have to accept their religion and all that this involved. But could she do this in all honesty?

Ray was watching her anxiously, so she smiled and stood up.

"Let's walk to the gate where you came in and then go back to see Aunt Emily. It's your turn now!"

He raised his brows in some concern as he joined her. "And the sun has gone," he said, as they crossed the grass to the lake where children shouted and sailed their boats. "But we are together, Leah. I can scarcely believe the wonder of it?"

She nodded, aware, too, of a happiness that could almost banish her worries. When they reached Ray's car, he handed her a parcel, lightly wrapped. Inside, she found the lovely carved bowl she had admired at the fete. "It's beautiful. Thank you, Ray. I'll treasure this always."

On their arrival at Aunt Emily's house, she came out and greeted Ray kindly but with a certain reserve.

"Young man," she said, giving him a close scrutiny. "I'm not sure that I should be welcoming you at all." But Leah recognised an indulgent light in her eyes.

To her further relief, her aunt and Ray soon found they had much in common as both had been reared in country districts. Aunt Emily was interested to hear of Ray's Massey-Harris binder and

Fordson tractor and the work he had been doing. She was glad to hear his cows were still being milked by hand. She felt doubtful about some of the new farming methods where milking was done by machines and laying hens were kept in cages. Ray told her of his sister, Louise, whose work with poultry and gardening was more to her liking.

In the dining room, looking out on the remains of Aunt Emily's roses and Michaelmas daisies, they had a pleasant meal of salad and ham, scones and fresh cream sandwich, made by Leah. Later, when the time came for Ray to go, Aunt Emily left them together.

Ray held her close and told her how much she meant to him, and Leah had no thoughts beyond these precious moments, this happiness they had found together.

"Thank you so much for having me here," Ray told her aunt as she joined them at the front door. "This has been a very happy day for me. But I am aware that my presence here can only bring unhappiness to Leah's parents."

Aunt Emily nodded anxiously. But soon she managed a smile.

"And you'll be back here, I'm sure - no matter what I might say." She stood with Leah, waving, until Ray's blue Austin car had vanished.

"Dear child," she said, shaking her head uneasily, "what a dilemma you have landed us all in! But when I see those stars in your eyes, what can I do about it?"

During the following weeks, Ray arrived to see Leah most Sunday afternoons, and they went walking or driving round the coast. Leah had decided she would not visit his mother and sister until the new year.

One Sunday when Ray was absent, Aunt Emily suddenly asked: "Have you and Ray discussed the question of religion, Leah?"

"There's no hurry about that," Leah said defensively.

"Well - it's not something you can decide overnight. I'm sure Ray hopes you will become a member of his Church. And for someone reared as you have been, that would be a big step to take. Don't you think the pair of you should discuss this very soon?

Leah's thoughts began to struggle with her aunt's suggestion - on the one subject she kept trying to avoid. Ray's Church and his religious life seemed so complicated compared with her own upbringing and attendance at their unadorned little church hall.

Yet these same differences had existed between herself and her great friend, Helen Burke, with whom she was now happily corresponding. Helen had spoken of her attendance at Mass, of confession, Holy Water, the Eucharist and other sacraments. Like Helen's Irish dancing, Leah had considered these religious observances as just another separate area of Helen's life, and certainly no threat to their friendship. So why could it not be the same between Ray and herself?

Aunt Emily sounded serious as she continued: "What will happen, Leah, if you find yourself unable to accept some of the traditional rituals of the Catholic Church? You are your father's daughter in more ways than you think. And you must remember that what can be ignored in friendship, could become of great importance in marriage."

In her heart, Leah knew her aunt was right. If she wished to share Ray's life, she must discuss those matters that meant so much to him and his family.

During the few weeks before Christmas, the weather grew more wintry, and Leah and Ray often remained at Aunt Emily's log and coal fire. Her aunt often visited an elderly friend at this time and took her a few of the fresh eggs brought by Ray. Leah would look through the bookcase and read extracts to Ray from some of her favourite authors. The books of prose and poetry from her cousin's school days were the same as those she had studied herself.

It pleased her to see Ray's recognition and approval of some of her favourite lines from Tennyson's 'Lotus Eaters' or the 'Stolen Child' by W.B.Yeats. When she mentioned Gerard Manley Hopkins, he smiled and quoted: "Glory be to God for dappled things." Often his voice joined in as she read from the powerful and descriptive passages of Scott's 'Marmion' and 'The Lady of the Lake'. A few lines from the latter she read quietly again:

'And hope is brightest when it dawns from fears . . .

And love is loveliest when embalmed in tears.'

The words touched her deeply and brought a certain comfort to the disturbed corners of her mind.

Sometimes, she and Ray discussed novels they had read and the time just flew. Leah also read aloud from Dickens' novel, 'Great Expectations' and the exciting and dramatic events became an added attraction for their meetings.

Ray brought books from his home for Leah to read during the week: a play by J. M. Synge, 'Riders to the Sea'; 'Twenty Years Agrowing' by Maurice O'Sullivan, novels by Sean O'Casey and Walter Mackin; short stories by Frank O'Connor and other Irish writers. She began to feel the attraction and interest of Ray's cultural heritage. But her wider knowledge of these matters often deepened her anxiety about their future together.

Soon she must try to explain these fears to Ray. But would he find it difficult to understand?

When the weather permitted, they walked together on the shore, often under a cool, clear sky and pale sunshine. Happiness could be the finding of an attractive shell or stone, a late wind-swept flower or just to watch the restless waves, feel the gentle dampness from a bouquet of spray and listen to the sounds of Nature all around them.

On one such afternoon as the determined tide swept foaming in, Leah knew she, too, must show an equal strength of purpose and tackle the difficulties that surely lay ahead in a life with Ray and his people. She could only hope the outcome would match that of the waves, as she watched them retreating like liquid silk trailing a few loose, rattling stones.

She had found the courage to face her parents; now she must tell Ray of her troubled thoughts regarding their future together. She could only pray that the outcome would be happier.

Back in the car, hearing the muted cries of sea-birds and rocked by a whistling wind from the shore, she told Ray of her father's family upset as recounted by Aunt Emily. She said she knew from his reaction to this that her father would never change his views about Ray's religion, never accept him into the family.

"He is filled with bitterness," she said, "something I do not share or even understand. But I am troubled, knowing I would find it difficult to accept some of the beliefs and practices of your church."

"I think you are worrying too much about these matters," Ray told her. "I was hoping that your unhappiness with your father's religious beliefs might make it easier for you to accept the spiritual comfort that we find in our church."

Leah sighed. She had her own simple theory of a Christian way of life. Besides, to join Ray's church would sever completely any

68

hope she might have of a reconciliation with her parents, perhaps leave her in a constant state of guilt and remorse, something she felt she could never face. She gave Ray a rueful smile. "What are we going to do?"

"We're going to talk - we must," Ray said, in his usual calm manner. "There's nothing to be alarmed about. My religion is a way of life that has brought hope and contentment to people for centuries. It is a tradition among us that we make our church an attractive place. All our rituals and practices help to create an atmosphere of caring and this can bring comfort and an uplifting of the spirit. So attendance at church has become an essential part of our lives. There's nothing to be afraid of, Leah." He reached out a hand and covered her tightly locked fingers.

"Please - don't worry so much about this. No-one expects you to make such a great change in your life without preparation and help. Very soon we can arrange for our Parish priest, Father McManus, to talk to you. He is a very kind and understanding man."

"Could you become a Protestant, Ray?" Leah asked.

He shook his head. "I am the person you know, Leah, because of my religion. You, on the other hand, have found your own Christian beliefs, based partly on your upbringing and later decisions you have come to through your own thinking. My people have never wavered from certain forms of worship. From these I have received strength and courage, and an attitude of mind to face up bravely to the difficulties of life."

Leah knew that Ray's faith had helped him through the shock of his father's death and his sudden responsibilities for the farm and family.

She said, quietly, "Do you pray for us?"

"Of course, Leah," he said. "And I know that you pray, too."

"You see, Leah, there isn't much difference in the real heart of any true Christian faith. I can only hope that in time you will come to accept our forms of worship as a means of comfort and thanksgiving."

Leah knew Ray meant in time for their marriage in his church, among his people, one year away in January. She also knew he had spoken to Father McManus for guidance. But just now, her guidance must come from herself and from her daily prayers. Muriel had told her that if she did not accept Ray's religion in its entirety, her marriage would have to take place in the sacristy and not in the main church.

In January, when she would be twenty, she and Ray hoped to become engaged. She had felt happy and excited about this next stage in their relationship. But sometimes little stabs of fear made her send up a silent prayer that nothing would come to mar the happiness they were building up together.

With Christmas less than two weeks away Leah was helping her aunt with the cooking and preparations. Her cousin, Jane, and baby were coming to stay for a few days. Jane's husband, John, would return home after their Christmas dinner to see to his farm.

Leah thought often of her parents these days and was somewhat relieved when her aunt, while shopping in the city, called to see them.

"Your mother, of course, looks thin and worried, Leah. Your father was out at one of his meetings, as I had hoped. But Margaret seemed really pleased to see me. She put on the kettle right away and soon brought in some tea and her special date and flake-meal biscuits. It seemed almost like old times. I feel sure your father stopped her from answering our letters."

Her aunt looked thoughtfully at Leah. "I'm afraid, dear, your mother is still hopeful that you'll see the error of your ways - and return to them. I had to be brave and warn her that this might not happen."

"I also told her that Ray was a fine young man whose friendship could do you no harm. She made no comment to this - just rattled the cups on the tray and went off to the kitchen. All the same, I think I have eased her mind a little about you."

Leah felt much happier now about the coming Christmas period than she had thought possible. She sent her parents a card with a few words of love and greetings, although she did not expect a return message.

On the last day at work, Leah joined her two office friends for a meal out and afterwards they attended a concert in their church hall. Earlier in the week, she and Aunt Emily had seen the Nativity play in the local school and the following night had enjoyed a musical evening in the town hall.

The Christmas atmosphere was everywhere as they walked home through the town; decorated trees shone out their coloured lights

70

from many windows, and the familiar notes of songs and carols reached them on the chill night air.

Leah put up their own decorations and parcelled the last of her presents. For her aunt she had bought a small portable radio set. For Ray, she had knitted a chunky green pullover in cable stitch. She hoped Muriel would like her jumper knitted with blue angora wool. She had already received perfume, 'Nuit de Paris', and a silk patterned scarf from Muriel, brought by Ray.

Leah had seen Muriel a few times since the summer. She drove occasionally to the sea-side town and brought Leah up to date with her own and all the country news. Aunt Emily was having a 'phone installed before Muriel's wedding. She said it would help to keep her in touch with her own daughters. But Leah knew her aunt had given thought to her, too, so that she could reach both Ray and Muriel any time.

Leah's friend, Jenny, from the city, had now departed to a job in England, but they wrote to each other occasionally and hoped to meet during the summer.

When her aunt's visitors arrived, Leah was greatly attracted to Jane's chubby baby Adam with his wispy curls and blue eyes. Now several months old, he was taking a great interest in his new surroundings. He could also set up screaming sessions when conditions were not to his liking. But it was a joy to cuddle this soft little bundle asleep in her arms while his mother and grandmother prepared the family Moses basket with its flowered and frilled coverings.

This was the first baby that Leah had ever held or even seen at close quarters. Soon she was wheeling him in his low pram up and down the sheltered garden to put him to sleep. Later, when she was left with Adam in his bath, she felt extremely nervous as he joyously flailed the water with legs and arms. Jane only laughed and said it was good practice for her.

The first time she lifted him from his bath, then struggled to dry, powder and dress him, she was exhausted. Putting in the nappy pins safely seemed a most hazardous job. But at last she was able to press her face close to his and feel the light, snuffly breath and the soft petal skin with its powdery scent.

As arranged, Ray joined them on Christmas day and he and John got on well together, exchanging views on the weather and prices of cattle against feeding costs among other interests.

Jane, with a mischievous look, put the baby on Ray's knee and his eyes widened in alarm. Like Leah, he had little knowledge of handling babies, but he soon became intrigued having his fingers gripped tightly by this new little person with his comical three-toothed smile and sudden vocal noises.

Aunt Emily remarked that Ray was more used to young farm animals like a baby calf that could manage, with a bit of a wobble, to stand and even walk a little in the first few minutes of life.

How quiet the house seemed when everyone had left. Then it was back to work for Leah. Her aunt had recently retired and now it was very pleasant to return on cold evenings to find a warm fire burning and their meal ready.

These early days of January were filled also with anxious moments, for Ray was taking Leah to see his mother and sister before Leah's twentieth birthday and the announcement of their engagement. As she considered her possible future life with Ray, Leah knew this meeting would certainly be vital.

EIGHT

On the Sunday of Leah's visit to the country, she was in a fever of concern. Outside, the path and road were clean and dry, swept by a biting wind. All traces of the night's frost had gone and the sun was shining, surely a good omen for the meeting today?

She brushed and combed her hair carefully, then pinned it back to each side, trying to control the more unruly curls in an effort to appear fully grown-up and sensible looking. She chose to wear the fine woollen dress in a pretty shade of lavender that Ray had admired. It had a slightly flared skirt and cream embroidered collar and cuffs. She slipped on Ray's Christmas present, a dainty gold watch that now replaced the childish model she had worn for some years and was no longer reliable.

Finally, she put on her new coat, a present from Aunt Emily. It was a warmly-lined, belted, olive-green waterproof with lighter toned trimmings and was the most stylish coat she had ever possessed.

Ray's smile, as he drove up to the door where she stood ready, showed undisguised approval of her appearance. And this helped to increase her confidence. But as they drove out into the country, with sleet hitting the windscreen from a darkened sky, Leah began to feel more and more apprehensive.

Ray tried to divert her thoughts with messages from Muriel and other items of country news including Jim's continued attendance around the dance-halls - much to the disapproval of his parents. But she was scarcely listening.

Leah knew that Ray's family were ready to welcome her as his future wife. She knew also that, like Ray, they hoped she would accept their Catholic religion - for assured family unity and happiness. Their parish priest, Ray had said, would give her every help and instruction. But today's visit was simply to meet and get to know Ray's immediate family.

As they approached the village, the sky was clearing and the rain had stopped. Ray pointed out some of the Anderson fields that bordered the roadside and where later he hoped to be ploughing and sowing crops. Beyond the house, Leah saw a group of cows sheltering beside a large corrugated iron hay-shed.

A small plantation of bare trees, darkly silhouetted against the clouds, momentarily hid the grey house just up from the road. Leah held her breath as they turned in past the low privet hedge of the bungalow to their left. Her heart did strange things as the car swung to the right and drew up at the glass porch of Ray's home.

She stared ahead for several seconds, seeing only a bleak-looking orchard of damp trees, their branches green-coated. Ray touched her hand in a gesture of encouragement before getting out. Soon she was beside him, legs unsteady as she went forward to meet a tallish, slightly-built woman whose dark hair had a swathe of white across her brow.

"I've been looking forward to meeting you," Mrs Anderson said in a low voice. Her solemn, dark eyes held Leah's a little warily as they shook hands.

Louise, who had been standing near, now came forward and greeted Leah with a quick, nervous smile. Her heavy dark hair, combed into a bun at the back and her thin, anxious face, made her appear older than her twenty-seven years. As they all moved into the hall, past pots of ferns and geraniums, she took Leah's coat with an admiring glance and hung it away.

In the sitting-room, a lovely log fire threw flickering shadows on walls and pictures, on comfortable-looking upholstered chairs, a polished table and ornaments. When everyone was seated, Louise and her mother asked about the journey and the state of the roads. Leah's aunt was mentioned and they spoke of her kindness to Ray. Leah then thanked them for the gifts they had sent from the farm.

Outside, the late afternoon sky was darkening rapidly and Leah felt disappointed when Louise switched on the lights. She now pointed out two or three family portraits, enlargements, she said, of small snapshots. The work had been done very expertly through a businessman who had called around the houses for orders, several years previously.

Louise then shyly produced some needlework and knitting she and her mother liked to do on winter evenings. Her embroidery of lilac flowers on unbleached linen and her crochet work on table mats were beautifully executed. Leah became so interested she scarcely noticed when Ray left the room to see to outside work. His mother soon followed, stating quietly that there were things needing attention in the kitchen.

Louise admired Leah's dress which she had made with help from Aunt Emily. She also asked about her work and life in the seaside town. Was she fond of animals and country life in general? Did she do much gardening, cooking, sewing . . .?

Leah could see that Louise considered it important for a farmer's wife to know something of these matters. And she felt grateful to her mother, her aunt and the Lintons for her knowledge, not only of house-keeping but of the farming world. A thought came to her that perhaps one's life was preordained - each stage a preparation for what was to come. That is, if you followed the teaching of God . . . A pang of guilt ran through her as she recalled the words of the Bible: 'Honour thy father and thy mother . . .' Confused and anxious, she tried to give attention to Louise who appeared to be more relaxed now that it seemed her brother's choice of wife might not be entirely unsuitable.

When Ray and his mother returned, Louise went off to see to the evening meal. Ray opened a drawer and handed out photographs of the family at various ages, while his mother attended to the fire and added an occasional remark about the time and place when the snapshots were taken. When Leah saw the two older sisters at their convent and Father Stephen, in his clerical clothes, standing with his mother outside their front door, she grew anxious again.

Then Louise called them to come to the dining room. This smaller room looked out on the silent winter darkness of the back garden until Louise drew the curtains. Muriel had told Leah of all the flowers, fruit and vegetables that flourished there in the summer - mainly looked after by Louise.

They took their seats at a round table covered by a white linen cloth, edged with a deep border of lace, the work of Ray's mother. Soon Louise served out portions of a steak and onion pie, most tempting with its appetising smells. Vegetables were handed round and everyone was busy. The dessert that followed of home-preserved plums, pink blanc-mange and whipped cream was equally enjoyable.

When their coffee was finished, Louise showed Leah over the four-bedroomed house and told her of its history and the building on of its second story by her grandfather.

It was a pleasant, well-kept home but, at that moment, it seemed quite remote from Leah's life. She found it impossible to imagine herself having any part in its running, especially with two such competent house-keepers already in possession.

As they walked around, she was reminded of her friend Helen's home where she had seen similar holy pictures, little statuettes and a receptacle of holy water in the hall. Again, she felt disturbed, remembering her father's disapproving voice, his cold eyes warning her sternly against any close association with such a family.

Shortly after this, she and Ray prepared to leave for their promised call with the Lintons. It was very dark now with rain beginning to fall as Leah said goodbye and thanked Ray's mother for having her.

"We hope to see you soon again," Louise called from the lighted doorway. As Ray swung the car round, she waved vigorously. Their mother stood quietly watching, her face partly in shadow. Then her hand rose slowly in a more delicate gesture of farewell. Leah had a feeling that Ray's mother could not quite see her as the next Mrs Anderson - a position she found difficult to imagine for herself.

"Not too terrible, was it?" Ray remarked as they drove out to the road. "You certainly made a hit with Louise."

"I like her very much," Leah said. Then she sighed. "But I don't think your mother is very happy about me. She was kind, I know, but I noticed she rarely smiled. And her thoughts seemed to be elsewhere."

"You mustn't think anything of that," Ray said, hurriedly. "Mother has been - well, somewhat withdrawn from us all since Father's death. But she's still keenly interested in everything. I'm sure she will try to help us in any way she can."

Lights streamed out from the Lintons' house and they received a boisterous welcome as they dashed through rain from the car. Tom was there, too, standing behind Jim who seemed, for him, rather subdued. Leah could see that the whole family were facing the fact that she and Ray did not intend to be parted, that this visit to the family home had set the seal on their continued relationship. She noticed how their eyes rested on Ray and herself with obvious interest and a certain concern.

Muriel soon took Leah away, ostensibly to show some wedding gifts she and Tom had already received. "I'm dying to know how you got on with Ray's mother."

Leah smiled. "Everything went very well. I've really had a lovely time." Not even to Muriel would she voice her private fears.

"And do you and Ray intend to go ahead with your engagement?"

"Of course we do. Surely you know that?"

"And have you decided what to do - about the question of religion?"

"Don't rush me," Leah said. "Even Ray isn't doing that."

Muriel looked contrite. "I'm sorry, Leah - it's just that I truly want you both to be happy."

After a quick cup of tea, Leah and Ray were on their way again. Frost had been forecast for later on, but now flurries of snow were slanting through the lights of the headlamps and melting into the dampness everywhere. Yet, for Leah, this first journey driving with Ray through winter darkness held something magical. He told her of severe winters they had weathered on the farm during his father's time; of storms and river floods and cattle marooned; of frozen land and sheep dug out of snow.

They passed under an overhanging canopy of trees and Leah quoted two remembered lines from school days:

"Oh dreamy, gloomy, friendly trees,
I came along your narrow track . . ."

Ray gave her a quick smile. "Happy?" he asked.

She nodded. The countryside in all its moods intrigued her; this was where she felt she truly belonged - and with Ray. Of that she had no doubts.

Back at Aunt Emily's before midnight, the air now had the bite of frost. Leah wished Ray a safe journey home before the roads turned icy.

It was now her aunt's turn to ask how she had got on with Ray's people and Leah was soon recounting some of the high-lights of her visit.

But Aunt Emily interrupted: "Leah - I really meant - how do you feel about a possible future life with Ray's family?"

"The future is in God's hands," Leah told her aunt, dismissively, but with the trace of a smile. She didn't want to talk or even think about such things. The day had brought much happiness, too. She thanked her aunt for waiting up and said goodnight.

The next excitement was Leah's twentieth birthday and her engagement to Ray. All that afternoon the sun shone quite warmly and, after Ray arrived, they drove out of the town and walked on their favourite stretch of shore where the sea was gently lapping under a cool breeze.

Before today Leah had never worn a ring, not even at Hallowe'en or from a Christmas cracker. Her father had frowned on such frivolities. This narrow, gold band that Ray had placed on her finger was very precious - a symbol of his love and regard. She gazed often at the flashing colours from the single diamond in its platinum setting and felt strangely moved, recognising the promise it held of their deeper attachment to come.

In the evening they dined out early, taking Aunt Emily who had been persuaded to join them. Despite her jolly mood and obvious enjoyment of the meal - Melon and grapefruit cocktail, Fillet of Beef Wellington, Broccoli Hollandaise and creamed potatoes, followed by hot mince-pies and coffee - Leah guessed her aunt was deeply worried about her part in aiding them with their plans. And she would feel it was her duty to tell her sister of their engagement.

She had spoken to Leah that morning: "How can I condemn this friendship between you and Ray when it seems so right, so truly happy? I can only hope and pray that prejudice and man-made rules will not spoil things for you both."

When Aunt Emily had left to join some friends, Leah and Ray hurried hand-in-hand through the lighted streets to see a musical show. It was 'The Desert Song' being put on by a local repertory company. And all through the exciting events of the colourful story with its romantic music, Leah quite forgot the shadow of her estrangement with her parents. It would be all the deeper now with the news that she and Ray had taken a further step towards marriage.

As they slowly made their way out with the crowd, Leah knew that feelings of distress regarding her parents would rarely leave her unless she could, in some way, ease her alienation from them.

That night, after Ray had left and they had exchanged words of life-long love and devotion, Leah knelt and prayed earnestly that somehow, some time, she might be able to bring a little happiness to her parents. She prayed also that Ray and his family would have patience with her and understand her problems.

Soon Ray's springtime work on the land began in real earnest. And Muriel's wedding was only a few weeks away. Both he and Muriel could now reach her by 'phone so Leah was ready when Muriel arrived to take her back to the country for a fitting of the dresses. Earlier, in the city, they had chosen the materials and patterns and later had their first fitting with the village dressmaker, Mrs Bell.

On arrival, they found Muriel's cousin, dainty dark-haired Christine, who was to be Muriel's matron-of-honour, having a row of pins inserted down the seams of her long, blue taffeta dress. Leah had met Christine once or twice and also her husband and children. They lived above their green-grocer's shop in the local town.

"See how thin I'm getting!" Christine complained, slipping back into her skirt and jumper. "That's from running after the twins and hauling boxes of vegetables and fruit from place to place. Now I must dash - but I love the dresses - and you'll look a picture, Muriel."

Leah and Muriel now stood in their finery for Mrs Bell's inspection and, when Mrs Linton joined them there was much laughter and comment. Leah stood back to admire Muriel's white satin gown with its deeply frilled neck-line and cuffs. "Just beautiful," she said. "You'll look terrific."

Muriel swung her shoulders from side to side in her usual pretence of showing off. "Just wait till you see me with all the accessories and my hair newly permed - to say nothing of having my two attendants beside me looking so angelic, thanks to Mrs Bell."

Leah and Muriel now decided to accompany Ray and Tom for a drive into the country for parts of machinery they had left at the forge for repair. While the men chatted to the blacksmith, Leah suggested a walk down to a nearby lough. Here they saw alder and willow catkins growing on the bushes at the edge and reflected in the water. On a sheltered bank, a few early primroses were peeping through.

A dark-feathered water-hen with a red bill and a white patch under its tail rushed squawking from some reeds. It swam on past them, head and tail jerking rapidly. They found its nest among the reeds. It contained one egg, buff in colour with reddish-brown speckles.

This springtime re-awakening of Nature, so fresh and beautiful, gave Leah a feeling of hope and happiness for the days to come. Muriel, too, was in great form, excited about her wedding and eager to discuss their latest plans.

"Tom and I are hoping to have an extra living-room built on to the Coulter house - for a bit of privacy. It's something you and Ray could consider for yourselves."

"I don't think Mrs Anderson would approve of that," Leah said. She was hoping that Ray's mother would not be quite so unfriendly as Mrs Coulter. But she was anxious, all the same.

Back at the Linton house, Leah was reminded of other days in the big bright kitchen with its appetising smells of fresh cooking and Mrs Linton happily in charge. Soon they were all enjoying the favourite evening meal of fried bacon, eggs and potato bread, while they also engaged in lively talk of farming and the local gossip.

Later, Jim, who had taken to playing the accordion, was asked to give them a tune or two. With great verve, he started off with: 'If you're Irish come into the parlour . . .' And everyone clapped. Then he played: 'When I grow too old to dream, I'll have you to remember.' He sang the words softly and winked at Leah giving her his audacious grin. This made her smile. They all knew Jim by now; nobody took him seriously.

Before leaving Leah home, Ray took her for a brief visit to his mother who asked her to come soon for a longer stay and to see Louise who was absent that day.

As they drove away, Ray said he would like to show Leah the church his family attended which many of the country people still called the 'chapel'.

They soon turned off the main road and Leah saw it at once on the hillside, stone built and venerable-looking in the evening light, and very like the church in the village. Above the door was a small bell-tower. Ray told her the bell needed repair and had not been rung for some time.

Leah fell silent as they approached the unlocked door past graves and headstones, ancient yew trees and other ever-greens. Inside, it was cool and shadowy, except for colour in some stained-glass windows. Leah looked around nervously. She knew that thoughts about her parents were causing much of the beating fear inside her. Ray took her hand and smiled encouragement, and she walked beside him past confessional boxes draped with green curtains, groups of candles, a statue of the Virgin Mary in an alcove. The Bible scenes, depicted in mouldings along the wall, showed the Stations of the Cross, Ray told her.

She stood before the railed-off altar, similarly carved and draped in blue and gold as in Muriel's church. She sensed the peaceful, holy atmosphere that surely could be found in any church where people of true Christian faith gathered for worship.

And here in Ray's church, God willing, she would be married - if Ray could be granted the dispensation he needed from the Bishop. She knew this would be necessary unless she accepted Ray's religion in its entirety. But that was something she would never be able to do in all honesty - quite apart from her wish to spare the anguish of her parents as much as possible.

The news of her marriage would remove any hope they might have that she would change her mind and come home. And Leah felt she must hold on to some small link with her past and not cut completely the life-line to her own family, leaving them with only a bitter and resentful old age. There was just one tiny ray of hope that she might be able to bring them some happiness in the future. But for that she would have to wait and see.

During the next few weeks, Leah and Ray were both very conscious that they must come to terms with their religious differences. Leah could not give Ray any assurance that having talks with Father McManus would greatly alter the situation or help her, personally. While Ray seemed to understand her unhappiness over her parents and her unshakable belief in her own religious concepts, he said there were other vital considerations they must discuss.

He spoke of these, reluctantly and apologetically, one Sunday as they sat in a sheltered corner of Aunt Emily's garden. "We have

81

got to think of the religious upbringing of the children we may have, Leah."

"I understand," she said, thinking of the marriage of her father's sister . . . "I, too, hope we have children. And I know it would be most important in a family like yours that any boys should become members of the Catholic church."

She paused only for a moment. "But I would like to have a daughter to bring up in the Protestant faith - if we should be given a girl. You see I feel so guilty about hurting my parents, I long to ease their unhappiness. And to give them a grand-daughter reared in their own faith seems the only way." Leah gazed at some scarlet tulips waving in the breeze, at a friendly robin hopping near, and waited anxiously.

Ray seemed to be thinking rapidly. Then, having made up his mind, he said: "If this wish of yours means so much to you, Leah, perhaps something could be arranged." His smile was a little uncertain.

"You must consider that your parents might not welcome a daughter of mine. Anyway, we may not have a daughter."

"I'd have to accept that." Leah said. It meant her plan would come to nothing. But all that was in God's hands. "And supposing we have only girls." She gave Ray a challenging look now, suddenly confident that together they could face any difficulties.

"In that case," Ray said, giving her a quick smile and slipping an arm round her waist, "I'd remind any daughter of ours of what their mother had done and hope she would follow suit - and marry a fine young man of the Catholic faith!"

Now it had become like a game they were playing, although they both were still aware of the serious undertones. But always Leah felt sure that she and Ray had enough in common in their Christian beliefs and in their regard for each other to make a success of life together.

NINE

Easter time was barely over when Leah returned to the country for Muriel's wedding. This was her first experience of such an occasion and she was amazed at all the activity going on with people and parcels arriving and the endless making of tea. Even the stolid Muriel appeared somewhat flustered at times in the rush to have everything ready: reception and going-away arrangements checked; clothes packed; flowers for the church; thank-you notes . . . And Tom and his best-man, cousin Harry, had to be carefully instructed about their responsibilities.

But Muriel managed to take Leah to the Coulter farm where great changes were taking place. The new building for her egg-producing venture was soon to be fitted with rows of wire cages. She hoped to get started when her first batch of young Leghorn pullets would be about twenty weeks old. Each cage, she explained, would hold four birds. The floors of wire mesh would have trays below to facilitate cleaning, and the eggs would roll to a ledge, safely and cleanly. Dry food and water would be in little troughs at the front of the cages.

Leah wondered about the confining of hens in such small spaces, but Muriel said they would be quite happy to be well-cared for and fed.

"I hope to show you all this in action in the near future," she said, her eyes alight with enthusiasm. "And we'll be the first in the district to have this battery system. But now you must see our own new quarters, though they are far from finished. And we'd better call at the house or I'll be in trouble." She raised her eyebrows in a wary look. "I just hope Tom's father is around; I'm not exactly a favourite with his mother, I'm afraid."

At the side of the two-storey farm-house, Leah saw new brickwork in progress for the extra living-room and separate kitchen for Muriel and Tom, all of which, Muriel said, was regarded as totally unnecessary expense by Mrs Coulter. Tom's poor father was suffering much abuse for permitting and helping to finance these changes.

Leah had never met Tom's mother, but she had spoken to his father on one or two occasions when he had called at the Linton house for a lift to a fair or cattle sale with Jim and his father. Robert Coulter was in his late fifties, a quiet, pleasant man like Tom, only taller and more heavily built. His speech was slow, almost a drawl. Before answering any question or making a comment, Leah had noticed he fixed his gaze on some distant point as though seeking inspiration before committing himself.

"He's a dear," Muriel said. "But like poor Tom he has to watch his step at home for the sake of peace." She stopped suddenly, and shook her head.

"I shouldn't be going on like this about my future mother-in-law. The truth is - it's due to her unflagging industry and keeping the men to their work that the Coulters have got where they are. Jim and his Dad left on their own, are fairly easy-going. But Mrs Coulter's mottoes are: 'Never put off till tomorrow what you can do today', and 'Waste not want not.'"

"Well then," Leah joked, "the pair of you should get on well together!"

Muriel shrugged. "That remains to be seen."

They were about to cross the yard when Mrs Coulter appeared at the door of her little dairy some distance from the house.

"She keeps the milk there and makes butter for the family in a small table churn just like we do," Muriel whispered. "But I'm afraid it won't be someone like mother I'll be dealing with very soon."

As Mrs Coulter turned towards them, Leah saw she was of medium height, very thin, with short scrappy greyish hair. She was wearing a rather shapeless grey skirt and bottle-green jumper and she stood there, very straight, very stern-faced, gazing at Leah.

"So - you're the friend from the city," she said. "I suppose Muriel has been showing you her efforts to turn this place of ours upside down. There's nothing about here these days but noise - with dirt and bricks everywhere tripping us up. And we're throwing out good money for that!"

While Leah stood there speechless, Mrs Coulter's expression suddenly brightened. She looked away and called out: "Henry, Henry!" and a large tabby cat emerged from the garden hedge. Henry, Leah noticed, had a battered ear, an over-fat face and dark markings round one sinister looking eye.

As Henry ran towards his mistress, Muriel muttered: "He's her one soft spot. But, of course, he's useful about the place - chases all the rats and mice."

"Poor Henry hasn't been home for two nights. He wants something nice to eat. Don't you, boy?" Mrs Coulter was fondling the chubby head to his accompanying mews and stretchings of apparent appreciation.

"He knows what side his bread's buttered," Muriel put in, as Mrs Coulter made to move away with Henry purring loudly and impatiently about her legs.

Then she paused and gave Leah another searching look. "I hear you've got yourself mixed up with those Andersons at the bridge." She threw out a hand towards the village.

"God help your wit, girl. You don't know what you're taking on." She made a few disapproving noises and hurried away.

Leah felt her colour rising. She turned to Muriel who drew in her breath angrily and threw her eyes upward. "Take no notice of that one. You see, Leah, what I'm up against? Come on - let's go home. With luck, I'll see Tom tonight - but not tomorrow! Oh, dear - this is no time to be getting cold feet."

Muriel's and Tom's wedding day dawned cool and clear and, as the morning advanced, the sun came out and all was bustle and excitement in the Linton house as everyone got ready. Leah heard several cars passing into the village and groups of people hurrying on the road. Then their own car came and she and Christine were on their way.

The church was packed with quietly chatting guests and onlookers, all smiling and nodding in anticipation. Minutes later, the noise and murmuring suddenly faded as Muriel walked up the aisle on her father's arm to the notes of Wagner's Bridal March.

All through the singing and the prayers, Leah was carried away on a wave of emotion. Muriel had never looked so beautiful as she now stood in her white satin gown and flowing veil beside a handsome bridegroom, whom Leah scarcely recognised as Tom, in his sparkling white shirt and hired morning suit. She thought of Ray somewhere among the guests, she hoped, and perhaps feeling a little lonely in a strange church. Their own wedding the following January would be a much quieter affair and, in some quarters, would surely cause talk and excitement of a very different kind.

As the ceremony continued her eyes grew moist as she heard the quiet responses of Muriel and Tom to the minister's words in the hushed surroundings. And everywhere was bright and fresh-looking with urns of massed daffodils chosen by Muriel. The words of the hymn 'O Perfect Love' seemed to say everything possible for their future happiness. Leah found it difficult to control her voice as she sang:

"'Grant them the joy which brightens earthly sorrow;
Grant them the peace which calms all earthly strife . . .'"

After the Benediction came the notes of Mendelssohn's 'Wedding March'. Soon Leah heard movement around her and knew the ceremony was over.

Later, as they all piled into cars, Leah was able to relax a little as they sped away from the crowd of sight-seers at the church gates who were calling their good wishes and throwing rice and confetti.

The reception was at a hotel outside the town and Leah was soon caught up in the laughter and chatter all around, as she and Christine, Muriel and Tom were surrounded by guests including Ray. Drinks were handed out and everyone looked happy. Soon they all repaired to the dining room.

After an excellent meal - Mulligatawny soup, then chicken, ham and vegetables, followed by Pear Supreme - came the cutting of the splendid cake made by Muriel. Everyone was in merry mood during the speeches. Mr Linton's blue eyes smiled indulgently as he proposed the health of the newly-weds. Tom gave a quiet reply of thanks and proposed a toast to Leah and Christine as bridesmaid and matron-of-honour. The best-man's response on their behalf was followed by his reading of three telegrams that caused much laughter. Even Mrs Coulter sitting very erect in her sombre brown suit and hat allowed her face to relax a little.

The sun came out during the taking of photographs in the garden and Leah, seeing the family group being arranged, felt a stab of sadness. Unlike Muriel's parents, her mother and father would never stand smiling at *her* wedding.

When it came to saying goodbye, she and Muriel held each other for a moment, smiling, yet not very far from tears. As they rejoined the guests, Muriel looked very smart in her tan suit with pleated skirt, pill-box hat and cream accessories. Soon she and Tom, heads bent against the showers of confetti, raced for the car. They drove off, amidst much waving and calling of farewells, in Tom's second-hand blue Ford Popular. It had been draped with yards of yellow toilet-paper, while empty tins tied to the bumper were rattling furiously as the car disappeared from view.

Somewhere, round a few corners, all this decoration would be removed by Tom, Leah was assured and the happy couple would be on their way unencumbered for the short honeymoon on the North coast.

The following evening Leah returned to her aunt's house feeling a little sad, a little lonely. She and Ray had been to see Father McManus and talked at some length to the kindly parish priest, a small, middle-aged man who showed his concern about their problem. Leah had listened carefully to all he had explained to her and she had felt that the fundamental beliefs of their two faiths had much in common. But she had been unable to give him any assurance that even in time she could come to accept all the teachings of his church. She explained that this was the result of her own deep-rooted religious convictions as well as the upbringing she had had. Father McManus had been very understanding. He had said he would speak to his Bishop on their behalf.

Leah had scarcely settled back at the office when Muriel rang to say they were home again. She gave a brief account of their few happy days of freedom. The weather had been cool and showery at times, but they had enjoyed long walks in sunshine on mostly deserted sandy beaches with only the smell of seaweed, wild cries of sea-birds and the roar and splash of waves. They had been to a play called 'Boyd's Shop' and enjoyed it immensely. Muriel hoped that Leah would come to see them as soon as the builders had departed.

Spring turned quickly into summer, and Ray came early one Sunday to bring Leah to the country. They arrived in time for

87

lunch with Muriel and Tom in their new quarters, now completed. Leah could see how much they enjoyed having this room of their own. Simply furnished, it had a few wedding gifts on display and a coffee-table, hearth-rug and bookcase from Muriel's home. Even Mrs Coulter had given them two pictures of Highland scenes, also an armchair and some crockery.

Muriel had other news for Leah: eyes shining, she announced that she was expecting a baby at the end of January. "I'm afraid this means I may not be about on that very important day for you and Ray. But I'm hoping that Helen will be able to see you through."

Leah knew that the wedding ceremony would have to be quite short with no sacrament of the Mass - as she was not a member of Ray's church. But she hoped to be dressed as any other bride and was looking forward to getting her trousseau ready. While Tom and Ray walked round the farm, Leah and Muriel were busy discussing suitable materials for a winter wedding and all the necessities for Muriel's coming baby.

Later on, Leah and Ray left to have their evening meal with Louise and her mother. As Ray had received his dispensation from the Bishop for their marriage in January, Louise seemed anxious to show Leah everything to do with the running of the house. Leah had no doubt that both Louise and her mother hoped she would become a member of their Church in time.

"I think you and I could work very well together," Louise told her, opening store cupboards and showing bed and table linens.

Leah nodded and smiled her agreement, but she still felt most uncertain about her future in Ray's home. She could only do her best to avoid any family upsets.

When she asked Ray what he thought her domestic duties might be, he gave her a long, enigmatic smile. "I don't think you should worry about it," he said. "You'll see - everything will fall into place, sooner or later."

Leah continued to pray that this might be so. Ray's dismissive manner puzzled her. He was usually concerned about her difficulties. But she knew he had troubles of his own with all his outside responsibilities.

Leah had missed seeing Ray's brother Father Stephen, when he was home briefly at Christmas. He was soon to leave for South

America to work on the Missions. Some weeks later, he had sent Leah and Ray a very kind and understanding letter in which he wished them every happiness and said he prayed for them constantly.

Ray's sister, Eileen, had also written a most friendly letter to Leah. She told about their work and study at the convent for Missionary Sisters where some mornings they also helped Sister Housekeeper with the mending of sheets, towels, serviettes . . . They had a chalet by the sea for holiday times where they often bathed. And at night they went to sleep to the varying voices of the waves. She mentioned that some of the Sisters were soon to leave for Nigeria where the news was not very good. But, so far, all the Missionaries there were safe.

Eileen also gave a brief outline of the Sisters' years of preparation for their Missionary work. After leaving the Novitiate where they do training for two and a half years, they make First Profession for a further three years. This gives them an opportunity to examine the Religious Life to see if a Sister is suitable for such a life and whether or not the life is suitable for her. Only then is she allowed to make Final Profession. But first there are special classes in preparation that last for two months. Eileen explained that her sister, Kathleen, had just started her two months preparation to make Final Profession: the taking of vows for life. And during this time, it was not usual to write any letters. Eileen hoped that soon after this quiet period for Kathleen, which was like a Retreat, they would be home and could meet Leah.

Reading this letter gave Leah much to think about. She felt a great admiration for Ray's sisters who had chosen such a selfless and purposeful life and she was no longer so nervous about meeting them.

It was mid-summer when they came home and Ray arranged to bring Leah to the country one Sunday. But when she saw two nuns in flowing habits and head-dress sitting on the wooden seat in the front garden, she didn't feel so brave and could find nothing to say.

It was Eileen, all smiles, and looking so much like Louise who came forward to greet her. Kathleen, not so tall and somewhat paler, gazed at Leah and nodded briefly. Then she turned aside to smell some roses. When Ray went on to the house, Leah joined Eileen on the seat and soon they were talking like old friends about the family, the farm and people of the district. Kathleen had little to say; her few remarks were usually about the garden. When Eileen spoke quite openly of Leah's coming marriage to her brother, Kathleen remained silent. She bent over some plants, removing withered flowers and leaves with quick, impatient movements. But Leah could see she was watching and listening intently, her face grave and troubled. It seemed that Kathleen must be condemning her for ruining her brother's life.

Leah was relieved when Ray and Louise joined them and soon they all went into the house for tea with Mrs Anderson. Some time after this, Ray drove Leah home. He seemed quite happy about the afternoon meeting.

"I saw you got on well with the girls," he said.

"Well - I found Eileen so very like Louise," Leah replied.

"And Kathleen - more like mother," Ray put in with a knowing smile.

"She's certainly slower to make friends, more cautious. Many people about here have always thought Kathleen distant and even unfriendly. But she's not, really. Give her time, Leah."

But Leah felt that Kathleen could not help her feelings. In her eyes, Leah and Ray were going against all reason, all sensible teaching.

During Leah's absence that Sunday, Aunt Emily had driven to the city. She still kept in touch with her sister although Leah's father ignored her completely. But now her latest news made Leah feel just a little less cut off from her old home. For Aunt Emily reported that Leah's mother no longer hurried from the room when her daughter's name was mentioned. She sat quietly listening, her face sadly immobile, making no comment.

Leah knew she had hurt her parents beyond forgiveness. Yet she couldn't help wondering how their behaviour towards her could be called true Christianity - according to the Bible that her father read so assiduously. And this incongruity in her father's actions was something for which she could find no answer.

One Sunday when Ray arrived to see her, he came into the house at great speed, unable to hide his excitement.

"Have you won the Pools or something?" Aunt Emily asked.

"No - not quite that." He looked teasingly at Leah. "But you'll be pleased to hear this, too, I think."

"Oh, tell us quickly," Leah begged.

"Well, our elderly neighbours, Mr and Mrs Sloan, have been finding the country winters rather cold and lonely. So they are leaving our bungalow and returning to city life. And you and I, Leah, (D.V.), come January, can move into their house!" He lifted her high and swung her around. "Now - what do you think of that?"

"You knew - you knew about this all the time!" she challenged him, thumping his shoulders in mock anger and delight until he released her.

"Nothing was certain until yesterday," he insisted. "I knew this might happen, but I wanted to be sure."

"Well, I'm very pleased for you both," Aunt Emily told them. "And happening now, this gives you plenty of time. So I'll leave you to enjoy your good news and make plans."

Leah guessed that her aunt, like quite a few others, thought they needed all the good luck they could find.

All through the autumn Leah and Ray were busy most weekends with the renovation of the bungalow. Leah had learned to drive that summer and her aunt often lent her the car, so that Ray could get on with his work.

Having decided on colour schemes, they found someone from the village to do painting and papering. Several items of furniture and furnishings were bought from the previous tenants, and new articles for sitting-room and bedrooms were chosen in the town. Ray's mother helped them financially and gave them several things from the house. Leah thought she probably felt a sense of relief at not having to share her home with a strange daughter-in-law.

Aunt Emily arrived to see the bungalow and met both Ray's and Muriel's people. Leah longed to bring her mother, but it seemed *that* never could be possible. During these busy weeks, Leah and her aunt were also measuring, cutting and sewing yards of lovely white satin. Helen, who was now to be her bridesmaid, had helped to choose the materials. Her own gentian blue gown was being made up in the city. Both dresses would have mandarin necklines and full skirts.

By early December, with help from their friends, the bungalow was ready. Leah and Ray thought it looked beautiful as they lit fires and went from room to room admiring and rearranging things.

Earlier on, Ray and his young helper, Davy, had cut down an old ash tree that was blocking the light from the kitchen and they now had a good supply of logs ready in a large hand-made wicker basket. Ray's family had brought the basket from the West coast of Ireland when on holiday, years earlier.

One afternoon, Muriel, a little slower getting about these days but looking very healthy in a brightly-coloured maternity smock, showed them round her happily clucking battery hens. She said the egg-production was very good and her hens didn't seem to mind the confined quarters, artificial lighting and fans humming in the roof.

Muriel explained that although the feeding and cleaning were partly automatic there were still hundreds of eggs to be lifted each day, some to be cleaned, and then packed into boxes for transport. Tom and his father had undertaken to see to this work for a time when the baby arrived. She only hoped this event would not take place too early and keep her from the excitement of their wedding day.

Leah hoped so, too. Only a few close friends and relations would be present at the shortened ceremony, omitting the sacrament of the Mass. Afterwards, they would all drive to the outskirts of the town for the reception.

A few days later, Leah travelled to the city by bus to meet Helen and do some Christmas shopping. Everywhere was brightly lit and decorated; shops had splendid displays of goods as they hurried from place to place buying gifts. Leah was also looking for her going-away dress. She finally found a 'Susan Small' model in fine woollen material, of a light chocolate colour. The skirt hung in deep folds below a tunic-style top with long slender sleeves. Helen said it looked very smart and the colour was a perfect foil for Leah's flaxen hair.

Over a welcome meal, they discussed arrangements for the wedding and their next meeting in a few days when Leah and Ray hoped to join Helen and her friend Sean McCarroll to see 'Cinderella' at the Opera House. They then walked towards the City Hall to see the huge Christmas tree with its hundreds of lights. They stood listening to the Police band playing: 'Oh Come All Ye Faithful' and 'Silent Night'. The music was a lovely reminder of the true purpose of Christmas, and people were smiling at each other in appreciation and acknowledgement of this thought.

Soon it was time to meet Ray who was coming to drive Leah home to her aunt. She felt a sudden sadness, seeing Helen leaving to join her welcoming family - so near to her own old home - where no-one was waiting or watching for her.

Christmas day passed very quietly this time with no visitors. It seemed right not to desert Aunt Emily whose family were unable to come due to illness. Ray's aunt and uncle from County Kerry were staying at the Anderson home for a few days. Leah had met them with other members of the family. She had enjoyed her visit, yet she was still conscious of a certain reserve, a wariness between herself and Ray's relations.

With no job now to keep her mind occupied, Leah had moments of anxiety between bursts of excitement. The preparations for her wedding day had been seen to as far as possible and her dress hung ready in the wardrobe. It looked so grand, finished off so expertly by Aunt Emily and waiting there with the flowing veil and pearl-edged hair band. She could scarcely believe all this belonged to her, or that everything to do with it was real.

Recently, Aunt Emily had bought her first television set. "To keep me company, Leah, when you are gone." Soon they were both keenly watching a variety of programmes: News, Gardening, Hancock's Half-hour, Our Mutual Friend. A girl from Donegal, Bridie Gallagher, who had sung locally to much acclaim, had now appeared on a variety show at the London Palladium.

Sometimes the weather reports worried Leah, especially when she heard of fog, ice-bound roads and some places blocked by snow. Ray 'phoned constantly, assuring her that the road to Muldare was clear and safe, and reminding her of the few days left before she would be on her way to stay with the Lintons prior to their wedding.

Leah packed and repacked her possessions and finally the special dress was folded carefully in layers of tissue paper. The unknown future was rushing towards her. She felt a deep sadness saying goodbye to her aunt who had been so good to Ray and herself.

"Dear child - sure I'll be seeing you both in no time," Aunt Emily said. She gripped their hands tightly as she wished them a safe journey. Then she hustled them into the car. She stood waving, staring anxiously until they turned the corner out of sight.

TEN

On a cool, clear January day with sudden breaks of sunshine, just after Leah's twenty-first birthday, she and Ray were married. Father McManus officiated at the simplified service. Among the twenty or so guests, Leah's aunt and cousin Jane were her only relatives. Foolishly, Leah had hoped her mother might somehow appear. But that had only been wishful thinking.

Muriel's mother had helped Leah to dress and told her she looked a beautiful bride. She put her arms around her for a moment and wished her a long and happy life. Tears had filled Leah's eyes, knowing that her own parents would be far from celebrating the events of that day.

Happily, Muriel had arrived, a little out of breath, calling cheerfully: "Lucky is the bride whom the sun shines on," and pointing through the window to a stream of golden light across the fields. She looked rotund and rosy in a blue tent-like outfit topped by her mother's fox-fur.

"You won't be needing this, Mother," she announced happily, adjusting it snuggly round her neck. "Your beige coat has luxurious beaver edging to keep you warm."

Muriel turned Leah round, admiring her from every angle, kissed her lightly on the cheek and wished her every happiness. Then she hurried off to make sure her father was ready to act as Leah's guardian, now that he had been assured Leah's own father had no further interest in his daughter's life.

In the little country church, nothing seemed quite real to Leah, except that Helen was beside her, a picture in blue, and other friends were smiling encouragement. Then Ray stepped in beside her, giving her a look that stirred her heart and restored her confidence that all would be well.

As the ceremony proceeded, she listened gravely to the prayers and supplications, joining in where possible and feeling a sense of wonder and contentment enfolding her. Their promises to each other were given and the ring placed on her finger. Ray spoke out firmly and her own voice held only a trace of a tremor. Then it was all over and she and Ray were man and wife. She knew she must not let thoughts of her parents worry her, not today.

Later, as they moved out to the waiting cars, people were smiling in a kindly but questioning fashion as they watched them closely. Leah held tightly to Ray's arm, for the moment not worrying about anything, just happily content that her new life had begun and soon they would be away together.

On the journey to the country hotel, all through the reception, the few short speeches, the taking of photographs, Leah remained in this remote but strangely happy state. Even when she and Muriel noticed two of the guests glancing at Ray and herself and making grave, head-shaking comments, she accepted this as inevitable and was not upset.

"They're wondering how it will all work out between you and Ray, no matter how happy you both look today," Muriel whispered. "But they don't know you two."

Soon Leah stood changed and ready to leave in her new dress, camel-hair coat and brown velvet toque. Ray looked very smart in a herring-bone tweed top-coat as he smiled and nodded at joking comments from some of the guests. When he and Leah began to move away, there was a rush to follow them, a calling of good wishes, an onslaught of confetti. Then a cold wind, blowing through a line of cypress trees, made them all hunch their backs against the sudden chill in the air.

"Don't forget to send us a telegram if you have any big news," Leah called to Muriel from the shelter of the car. Then, with a final wave, they headed southwards towards the city of Dublin.

With a sense of relief that all the preliminaries were over, they smiled at each other with a sudden shyness. "Not too bad, was it?" Ray said, just as he had asked on Leah's first visit to his home.

She agreed. But now she had to ask Ray if he felt a little sad at not receiving the Sacrament of the Mass and the full blessing of his church on his marriage.

He said quietly: "We knew there would have to be sacrifices on both sides. You and I, Leah, can only pray for guidance in this life we have chosen." He smiled and reached out a consoling hand. "What happened today was the only way for us to make this possible."

As they raced along an almost empty road, talking, laughing excitedly and with Ray often bursting into song, it seemed they were on a great adventure. Several times the sky darkened and rain and wind buffeted the car. In a small market town they were held up for a time by a horse and its broken-down cart that had lost a wheel. But nothing could dampen the wonderful sense of freedom they felt, the feeling of achievement and, above all, their delirious happiness.

They approached the city in growing darkness, dazzled by all the lights. And now Leah began to feel a little anxious about the small hotel that Helen had recommended.

"You'll be quite convenient to theatres, museums, quaint little coffee houses and places you'll love to explore." Helen had been most enthusiastic and had given them a guide book showing the main attractions for tourists even in winter.

After many wrong turnings, they found the place in time to settle in before the evening meal. They had been given a front bedroom with a wide bay window, the only room in the small hotel to have a private bathroom. Leah looked a little anxiously at the large bed with its rose-coloured eiderdown, matching valance and shade on the bedside light.

"We're very grand, aren't we?" she told Ray as, hand in hand they stood looking out at the city, all lit up yet still dark and mysterious.

"We'll start exploring it all - tomorrow," Ray said, pulling her away. "But now there a a lovely cooking smell downstairs."

Three other guests were in the dining-room: an elderly Miss Hogan walking slowly with a stick and two business men talking earnestly of the day's happenings. They all nodded to each other and made one or two remarks. Then they settled down to enjoy their soup, roast beef and vegetables, apple-pie and cream and finally coffee.

Afterwards, as they spoke to the proprietress, Mrs Donnelly, a kindly, grey-haired woman, she gave them the usual meal-times for the next day.

"But no hurry in the morning - if you wish," she called after them with a smile, as they climbed the stairs.

They thanked her and said goodnight.

Leah finished her unpacking and then, as they made preparations to retire, she grew increasingly nervous and excited. Tonight held a special significance for them both. It was the culmination of a long and happy friendship. But, after tonight, there would be no turning back - no matter what might happen.

They knelt together and said their prayers. Leah prayed as usual for guidance in her new life and for forgiveness for causing the break-up in her home. Most fervently, she prayed that Ray would continue to love her - in spite of their differences.

As she got up, Ray took her hand. "You look very serious, darling. And this is our wedding night, remember?" His arms went round her and he held her close. Very soon, neither of them was giving the future any thought.

When Mrs Donnelly met them the next morning, her smile was very bright.

"I'm thinking you two are on your honeymoon," she said. "You just can't hide it. Sure it's shining out of your eyes. And may you never lose that look for each other."

Each morning, after a splendid breakfast of fried bacon, eggs and sausages, followed by toast and marmalade, Leah and Ray set out to walk through a nearby park or window-gaze around the shops. One or two mornings were frosty, sometimes it rained. Always, they ended up having steaming cups of coffee and cream cakes in a friendly little cafe before setting out to visit a museum or art gallery.

Two afternoons were spent among books and antiques in little secondhand places along the quays. Leah spotted a handsome green marble clock, priced at four pounds, ticking away happily. They bought it for their new sitting-room at the bungalow. When Ray told her to find something for herself, she chose a lovely silver brooch, an oval shape of leaves and flowers enclosing an amethyst stone the colour of violets.

Leah pinned it safely to her lapel, wondering about its previous owner and the story behind its being sold. Already it had become a special possession. For Ray, they chose a silver propelling pencil with a similar stone at the base. It was unusual and Ray was intrigued.

They paid one more visit to the quays and, after some bargaining, Ray secured for seven pounds ten shillings a beautifully carved barometer to hang in their hall. For four pounds they bought two fine silver candlesticks.

They also lingered among piles of books, delighted to find, often for a shilling or two, clean, new-looking volumes of poetry and prose by some of their favourite authors.

On their return each evening for an early dinner, Mrs Donnelly liked to hear of their adventures. She assured them they had not been robbed with their quayside purchases and she proved to be very helpful with suggestions for other outings and how to get there. Miss Hogan, sitting near, would nod and smile and sometimes offer her advice, pleased to be included in these friendly little exchanges.

One fine afternoon they drove to the Phoenix Park on the outskirts of the city. Here they found extensive parkland of gardens, fine buildings, sports grounds and a large zoological enclosure. They had been told to look out for the deer that roamed freely through the wide open spaces and among the trees. But that day, no deer were visible.

The evenings were exciting, too, when they visited shows in the city. On two occasions, with a sense of adventure, they found their way to little theatres in the suburbs where they saw 'Riders to the Sea' by J.M. Synge and 'The Shadow of a Gunman' by Sean O'Casey. For Leah, it was a very different world from schoolday plays like 'Cinderella' and 'The Mikado'.

Two days before leaving for home, a telegram arrived announcing the birth of a son to Muriel and Tom. Leah now gazed into the windows of 'Baby' shops and finally bought a blue pram suit and a rattle. Soon they were packing up all their purchases, delighted with everything yet knowing they had over-spent. They had had a wonderful holiday and Leah felt they would recall these happy days many times.

Their real, everyday life would be quite different, but they were both eager to start together in their new home.

Leah, always conscious of her mother's heartache, and that her father had completely disowned her, still clung to the thought that, in time, perhaps, she might be able to bring them some consolation.

On the long drive home they passed many farmlands looking damp and desolate with bare trees and fields, but Ray seemed undismayed and was full of plans and hopes for brighter days ahead. Leah spoke of helping Louise and getting their own garden into order. Then, in the early darkness, hearts thumping, smiling at each other, they drew up at the bungalow.

Lights shone out across the wintry flower-beds and Mrs Linton appeared at the door, arms wide to embrace them, calling words of welcome. She said Louise had just gone to close-up her hens for the night. She had left them groceries and some of her own baking, and Ray's mother was expecting them up at the house for supper.

Greetings over, Mrs Linton reminded Ray to carry his wife across the threshold to ensure good luck for the future. They were all laughing as he lifted Leah and set her down on their green settee in the sitting room near the glowing fire. Now they heard all the latest news: Muriel and baby - eight pounds, four ounces at birth - were both in excellent health and hoping to see them soon. Tom was quite the family man already and very proud of his son and heir. They would probably find Muriel up and about and back seeing to her poultry.

"She's a terrible wee girl for getting on with the work," Mrs Linton said, proudly.

Ray asked about Jim. Mrs Linton sighed. "He has taken up again with that Lindy Cummings girl. They were away dancing in the city Plaza at the weekend. We couldn't stop him. She's back working in their Post Office these days. If Jim marries that girl our place will go to wreck and ruin."

Leah said quickly: "Lindy's a happy, energetic girl and she probably knows more about farming than I do. Ray and I have often seen her helping on her uncle's farm."

"Well - maybe I'm worrying too much. Muriel speaks well of her, too."

But Mrs Linton was shaking her head as she lifted her coat. "Now I must go home. Louise and I have left you some things ready in the kitchen."

They thanked her for all her help and kindness, and she asked them to come and see her very soon. Ray rang his mother to say he and Leah would be with her shortly.

While he drove Mrs Linton the short distance home, Leah

opened cases and hung their clothes in the fresh-smelling wardrobes where Louise had placed little bags of lavender. She put away things in the spotless kitchen and then moved through the rooms unable to believe that it all belonged to Ray and herself. For the moment, she would enjoy that thought and think of nothing else. Smiling, she lifted the carved wooden bowl, her first present from Ray. Someone had filled it with apples and pears and she took a deep breath of their ripe, refreshing fragrance.

Then Ray returned and Louise arrived to bring them up to the house where she had the supper ready. Leah's new life was beginning.

During the days that followed it was very strange waking up to the ringing of an alarm-clock. In the past there had always been someone to waken Leah. Now she felt anxious that Ray should not be late starting the day's work with Davy who cycled in from the country in all weathers. These cold dark mornings, there was hay, straw and sometimes turnips to be got ready, meal given to the cows, milking to be done, byres cleaned out. Then many calves had to be fed and milk put into large cans and left at the road to be collected by the milk lorry.

Leah, safe in her easily kept house, had time to admire and arrange their wedding presents, to set up the marble clock and silver candlesticks now clean and shining, to watch snowdrops and crocuses pushing through the hard soil to colour the garden. But she wanted very much to be more useful, and was pleased when Louise suggested she might like to help with the poultry and rearing of young chickens, something she had a little knowledge of from her days with Muriel.

Each evening, she tried to have a nourishing and attractive meal ready for Ray so that he would not miss his family's splendid cooking. Sometimes, he was unavoidably late and her efforts were somewhat spoiled. But she thought of Mrs Linton, sympathetic and understanding, who met her husband with a smile even though the shepherd's pie was over-cooked, the rice-pudding brown and solid.

It was very pleasant occasionally to give little supper parties for friends and relations and to visit them in return. They went dining and dancing with Muriel and Tom and Ray's cousin Con and his wife Maureen to Farmers' Union nights in the local town hall. Muriel left the baby, in strict rotation, with her mother and mother-in-law. Mrs Coulter senior had taken greatly to her grandson, Robert. She even chased poor Henry when the child seemed in any danger from the over-friendly cat. But she was often critical of Muriel for not keeping the child warmly wrapped up in cold weather. Leah thought that Muriel was a splendid mother and Robert a beautiful baby.

"We had to call him Robert Samuel after his two grandfathers - for the sake of peace," Muriel explained. Granny Coulter nearly had a fit when I suggested names like Christopher and Trevor. She told me sharply it was time I knew that a first son was usually given a family name. Anyway, Tom and I are happy enough to call him Robert."

Most Sunday mornings Leah accompanied Ray and his family to their country church, but she remained seated while they went forward to receive the sacrament of the Eucharist.

At first, she received many disapproving and questioning looks from those around her, but gradually some of the congregation showed understanding of her position and how she felt she should try to cope with it. She also realised just how important this part of the service actually was for those brought up in the tradition of Ray's church.

Some Sunday evenings she went with Muriel and her mother to the village church where her presence also caused comment - and a few harsh looks. But for Leah it was important to keep in touch with her past life. Both Father McManus and the Reverend McKinney had shown great kindness and understanding.

"We are all God's children," the priest had told her. "That is all that really matters. And time may help you, child, to come to some decision."

But Leah could see that both men, although on friendly terms themselves, were perturbed and probably somewhat embarrassed by her divided loyalty.

On evening outings in the village - to a concert, a sale of work - Leah noticed a lack of her usual welcome from some church members.

"You see," Muriel explained, "your's is the first mixed-marriage in this Protestant place that they have had to deal with. And they're not sure how to handle the situation as they wonder if it is still correct for you to help at church functions as you have done in the past."

Leah was no longer sure herself. She only knew that she could close her eyes, and pray anywhere, at any time, inside or outside any church and feel that God was near, his presence the spur to making the necessary effort to help herself. But life, she had found, with so many man-made rules and prejudices was not always so easy or so simple.

ELEVEN

As the weather improved all was bustle and excitement on the farm. Ray and Davy were preparing fields for planting corn, wheat, potatoes, turnips and carrots. Leah hurried with her housework so that she could help Louise in the garden. She also tidied their own front flower-beds, soon to be bright with daffodils, polyanthus and pansies. And she thought of the two elderly people who had first planted the garden so hopefully.

With longer hours of sunshine, Leah liked to walk to the village for items of groceries and packets of seeds from the General Stores. Buds were appearing on trees and hedges; birds were building nests; primroses and bluebells began to line the roadside. Some people she met smiled and spoke of the weather, others she had known looked away. One or two, especially the stout woman from the first cottage, gave her cold and disapproving glances.

Ray said she must not let it trouble her. People felt uncertainty faced with a new situation. And it gave them something to talk about.

Sometimes Leah walked through the village to visit Muriel and little Robert. On one occasion, as Mrs Coulter, senior, passed the window, Muriel's expression became both comical and wary.

"I'm afraid our Granny isn't too pleased with us at the moment! You see, we've put a little bolt on the communicating door into her part of the house. Every time she heard Robert bawling, she came running in to lift him, complaining about the damage we were doing by letting him cry for so long! It was never more than a minute! And of course she was spoiling him. We explained to her that the bolt was just a precaution, a sign that we were getting the child to sleep and were afraid that any noise, even an opening door, might waken him again. Tom says she'll soon come round and, in the meantime, Henry the cat is getting a little more attention!"

These days, Leah's step was extra light and she gazed about her with a new sense of wonder. For it seemed fairly certain that, by October, she might be holding her own baby in her arms. So far, only Muriel had been told. And Ray had said they would wait until later to tell his mother.

Then shortly after Easter, on a Sunday afternoon, Leah and Ray walked up to the family home to meet some of his relations who had not been at their wedding. They arrived to find about a dozen people, mostly elderly, assembled in the sitting-room. Louise came forward to make the introductions and a battery of eyes were focused on Leah, making the anxious thumping of her heart change to plunging stops and starts.

She was wearing her going-away dress with her beloved antique brooch fastened at the collar. Her softly waving hair, newly washed and shining, was pinned tidily back. She reminded herself that Ray had told her, as they left the house, that he loved her dearly and was very proud of her. His words helped to keep her smiling among the truly friendly faces and the two or three others who remained tight-lipped and hostile looking.

One of these, a dark-haired young woman seated near the window, very smart-looking in a well-cut grey suit and pink blouse, gave Leah a long stony stare and then resumed her interest in the garden.

"Cousin Judith - home for Easter," Ray whispered. "Doesn't approve of me, I'm afraid."

Because of me, Leah thought, sadly.

Just then, a small white-haired stoutish man beamed a rosy smile towards them and announced across the room: "Well - I must say, young man, you've chosen a fine wee girl and no mistake. Good luck to you both - Ray boy!"

Amidst smiles and murmurs of agreement from some quarters, Ray quickly acknowledged these kind remarks and, taking Leah's hand, they moved through the guests to the elderly couple on the sofa near the fire.

"My great-aunt, Therese," Ray said, with a little bow.

Leah saw a bright-eyed, slightly stooped old lady who reached out and clasped Leah's hand warmly with smooth frail fingers.

"And great-uncle Dan!" Ray announced.

Leah shook hands with the jovial old man who had spoken out so kindly to them. He was the younger brother of Ray's paternal grandfather who had died recently, a year after his grandmother.

Just then Ray was called to hand round glasses of sherry and stronger drinks for some of the men and Leah found herself seated between the old couple. She felt more at ease now, and was soon listening to tales of Ray as a young boy and telling of her own days staying in the country.

A motherly-looking woman seated near tried to get Leah to accept - "A glass of something to bring more colour to your cheeks, dear?"

Leah smiled and shook her head. Already, the heavy odour of drinking in the room seemed over-powering, something she was not used to. Ray and his family were very light drinkers but it was the custom to be liberal when entertaining visitors. When many glasses had been refilled and again emptied, there was a further murmur of interest with the arrival of pots of tea, plates of sandwiches, cakes and a large cream-topped trifle in a cut-glass dish.

Leah hurried to help with a tray of food and was soon moving among the guests now busy exchanging family news and gossip that had little meaning for her. A thin, middle-aged man with a weather-beaten face was speaking of being on a pilgrimage with a party of people. Leah gathered that they had climbed a mountain in bare feet while fasting and praying. Leah's sudden presence caused a quick silence and an exchange of cautious looks between him and his companions. Then with a murmur of thanks they each reached out for a sandwich.

As she moved on, wondering about what she had heard, she approached Ray's aunt Peggy, keen-eyed and sandy-haired and with a cigarette clinging to the side of her mouth as she told his mother of her recent visit to somewhere called Lourdes. On noticing Leah, her voice trailed away, she smiled a little distantly and reached out to replenish her plate. Ray's mother did the same.

"I'm just an outsider here, an embarrassment to the family," Leah kept thinking to herself. There was so much she still did not know about the lives of Ray's people. And now the ache inside her was becoming tighter as she forced herself to approach the window seat. Here, cold-eyed cousin Judith was suddenly talking with great animation to her older companion about Ray's brother: "And Father Stephen is doing such valuable work on the Missions. His mother is mighty proud of him; we all are. It must be a consolation to her . . ." The speaker turned away pretending not to notice Leah's tentative offering of a plate of fairy cakes. Her companion, looking embarrassed, smiled at Leah and took one.

Deeply conscious of the rebuff she had just received, Leah made her way to the refreshment table, glad that most people had been attended to, but disappointed that Ray was no longer in the room. Louise handed her a cup of tea and a sandwich and said she, too, would have to see to things outside. Her mother had gone to make up a bed for the great-aunt and uncle who were staying the night.

"You can hold the fort, Leah. I won't be long."

Feeling tired and very lonely, Leah sat down by herself beside the table strewn with empty cups and the remains of the meal. She would have liked to rejoin the two friendly old people but they appeared to be ready for a few minutes sleep. Most of Ray's people, she felt sure, wished to show friendship. As Ray had said, she must try to understand their different cultural back-ground, their religious motivation.

But perhaps she was making too much of the present situation? Many young wives, like Muriel, were open to criticism from members of their husband's family. As snatches of conversation came to her, Leah knew it was no use deceiving herself; her own position among Ray's relations was a much more serious matter. At that moment she felt she was a complete outsider.

Now voices were growing louder, sometimes in such heated argument they frightened her. Perhaps this was how discussions among large family groups sometimes went on? But some people were staring in her direction! Her face grew cold; they must be talking about her.

To Leah's dismay, tears filled her eyes. And in great distress, she hurried from the room, deeply conscious of the sudden hush behind her.

In the empty kitchen, she stood weeping helplessly, feeling she had ruined everything for Ray and their future together. On his return, a few minutes later, she tried to tell him how she had let him down, disgraced herself and never again could she face his relations - never, never! And it seemed that nothing he said could console her.

When Louise came in, she stood staring in alarm at the unusual situation. Although not fully understanding what they tried to tell her, she was anxious to help and hurried off to tell the visitors that Leah was not feeling well and so she had advised Ray to take her home.

In a very short time she came rushing back, her eyes wide with happy speculation as they rested on Leah's tear-stained face.

"Great aunt Therese says," she reported breathlessly, "that Leah is well, she thinks - perhaps there's a baby on the way! And that would explain everything."

Leah, blushing, nodded and said that Aunt Therese was right. And, as Louise dashed back to tell the guests, Leah felt a surge of gratitude to Ray's elderly aunt for supplying an excuse for her strange behaviour, even though it was only part of the truth. But the old lady probably knew that, too.

Aunt Emily had warned Leah that marriage with Ray could bring many difficulties never encountered during their days of friendship. Yet Leah had felt confident that she and Ray would always be able to overcome the criticisms of the outside world and live happily together.

As they walked home, she tried to explain her sudden overwhelming feeling of not belonging among his relations. He had been right, she said, to want her to know more of his family's background and culture. If they should have a son, she could not bear to feel shut out, perhaps resented by her own child.

Ray tried to assure her that those who had been less than friendly were very much in the minority. In the weeks that followed he helped her to understand those aspects of his religion that were observed so faithfully by many of his people, and were essential to their mode of life and manner of worship.

Happy in her own more simple faith, Leah could see how welcoming, calming and supportive such observances could be to those brought up in that particular tradition.

When she and Ray were present for evening prayers with his mother and Louise, Leah found she could understand better now the purpose of the rosary beads, Stations of the Cross, confession and other traditional practices. Perhaps they were like music put to verse to make a song, or rhythmic steps to make a dance - and all to enhance their worth and attractiveness. But Ray assured her these religious practices held a deeper significance.

Always, Leah remembered that this form of worship had shaped Ray's life and nature and made him the person she loved and admired, whose basic principles in life so surprisingly matched those she herself tried to follow.

She was fully aware that their real difficulties would come from the outside world, especially with the birth of children. Yet the thought of their coming baby was a constant source of delight to both of them.

These were truly wonderful days as springtime merged towards the summer. With hours of sun and hours of rain, ploughed fields turned green again with growing crops, and grass for hay stood high, waving gently in the breeze. Buds on trees and hedges sprouted leaves overnight, or so it seemed to Leah watching from her kitchen window the miraculous changes taking place. A canopy of delicate green began to cover the bare branches of trees on the lane, so that the Anderson homestead gradually vanished from her sight. Only farmyard sounds remained.

In the front garden, pansies showed their cheeky faces beneath stately tulips. Lupins, pink and yellow, and white and purple foxgloves appeared against the bottom hedge. Soon summer scents of roses, lilac, lavender and the hum of insects filled the air on sunny days spreading happiness for Leah as she cut flowers for the house and brought in parsley and lettuce she had grown in their own garden.

Up at the farmhouse where, weeks earlier, she had watched pink and white blossoms in the orchard falling like confetti on the grass, now tiny apples and plums hung on the trees to grow and ripen until the autumn. When the blackcurrants and raspberries were ready for picking Leah helped to fill the cans and baskets, some for sale to local people and the rest to be made into jam.

In an adjacent field, the Rhode-Island pullets were quickly growing into egg-laying hens and on a fine day they could be heard singing a chorus of contentment as they searched the ground for grubs and other pickings. In hollows of dry soil under hedges, many of the fowl were dusting their feathers, obviously enjoying this contact with the earth.

Acres of hay had been mowed and saved during spells of fine weather. Tom, Jim, Ray and his cousin Con helped with each others' crops. The corn was cut with Tom's Massey Harris binder driven by Ray with his new Ferguson tractor. From the garden, Leah could watch some of the work being done. A patch of grain, flattened by stormy winds, had to be cut with a scythe. Then the sheaves were stooked in groups about the field to remain until well dried and ready to be stacked in the haggard behind the house.

Later in the year, a threshing machine would visit the various farms to separate the grain from the straw, assisted by helpers from around the village. Owners of larger farms in the district were engaging contractors with new machines called combine harvesters to cut their crops and fill the grain into sacks right away, with little manual help needed. Ray felt this method would suit only their larger fields.

Leah saw the farming life as a continuous cycle of work. With her greater knowledge of each season's contribution, so her wonder and admiration grew for the endless miracles of Nature.

She thought often of their own baby, due in a few weeks time and growing bigger and more active every day. It seemed to Leah that this making of a completely new little human must be the greatest miracle of all. She thanked God that her health had been good all along.

The district nurse and the doctor were both consulted from time to time. Muriel, of course, had her own advice: "Ignore all minor discomforts; they'll usually disappear if you watch what you eat and keep sensibly active."

Muriel's Robert was now sitting up in his pram, happily showing two front teeth as he bashed about with a rattle and an assortment of toys, sometimes sending them flying and then squealing with delight at the sight of poor Henry scampering for safety from this new ruthless enemy.

Muriel handed on to Leah a few of Robert's earlier garments, scarcely worn, including Chilprufe vests, romper suits and bootees. Romper suits, she was aware, were worn by baby boys and the thought made her heart beat faster.

Her supply of baby things was growing apace. By Michaelmas day she had a large drawer full of the necessary first-size garments, three of each; two dozen baby napkins; day and night dresses and several matinee coats she had knitted. Aunt Emily had almost finished a lovely woollen shawl and Louise was busy on a warm pram-suit.

So far, all the little garments were coloured white. Leah knew that while she and Ray would welcome either a son or a daughter, the arrival of a boy would naturally be greatly welcomed by Ray's family. Her own parents were never far from her thoughts at this time. Aunt Emily had said her mother seemed less strained these days and most eager to hear news of her daughter. Leah's father, on the other hand, still stubbornly ignored her existence, continuing his stoical ways to even greater lengths.

Soon Leah was aware that the clatter of machinery about the fields and farmyard had grown lighter, the colours in the hedges were brighter. And now she waited, her feelings both anxious and excited as the days slipped by.

TWELVE

On a fine afternoon in October Leah set out for the farmhouse. She walked up the back field, her feet rustling through leaves of varied shades of yellow, red and brown, some blown from the garden. Nearer the yard gate, a breeze stirred the branches of the great beech tree and a few more leaves came sailing down. Leah, although feeling extra heavy and awkward, hurried forward, reaching out eagerly until she trapped a flying scrap of yellow. Her success made her smile; to catch a falling leaf, she remembered from school-days, was sure to bring good luck.

As she wandered on by the hedge, admiring scarlet rose-hips, a fine spray of blackberries, she suddenly stopped. Somewhere inside her, she was aware of small niggling pains, recurring and fading. Alarmed now, and excited, she moved more quickly towards the house.

After 'phone calls had been made to nurse and doctor, Leah returned home with Ray and Louise. Some time later, when all preparations possible had been made, and Leah's pains were coming more rapidly, everyone felt great relief to see Mrs Hall arriving. Then the doctor came hurrying in to take charge and soon it was all over.

Leah heard lusty infant cries and was told she had a seven pounds four ounce baby boy, the picture of health. She was still sending up prayers of thankfulness when Louise and Ray came cautiously into the room and were soon fussing over the two of them.

That evening there was much rejoicing at the bungalow. Aunt Emily came to stay for a few days, and she and Louise couldn't stop admiring the dark-haired baby who, they said, already appeared to take notice of them. Ray's mother held her first grandson in her arms, gazing at him fondly and remarking how much he resembled his father. His blue eyes, she stated, would probably change to brown at a few months old - just as all her own children's had done.

Alone at last, Leah and Ray regarded their first-born in sheer delight and wonder, unable to take in that he truly belonged to them. They spoke of names that might suit him, but Leah decided the final choice should come from Ray.

After two more busy and exciting days with much 'phone ringing and people calling, Aunt Emily drove off early to do shopping in the city. Louise said she would call in at the bungalow as Ray had the vet coming and later would be away in the town.

It was mid-afternoon when Aunt Emily returned. Leah sat up quickly on seeing her standing at the bedroom door looking mysteriously bright-eyed.

"Leah," she said, "I've someone here who would like to see you - and the baby."

To Leah's amazement, she saw her mother, pale-faced and uncertain coming towards her. Noting the welcome in Leah's eyes, she reached out wordlessly for her daughter's hands, holding on to them tightly for some time, before bending down to kiss her cheek. Her eyes were full of tears as she turned to the cot and gazed down at the sleeping child.

"He's - a beautiful little boy," she said, her voice breaking. And Leah smiled through her own tears as her mother gently lifted the child and held him close for some time.

Aunt Emily began quickly to open parcels they had brought and hold up little garments and presents for Leah. The arrival of Louise was a further happy diversion and soon they were talking together about poultry rearing and harvest work. Leah's mother mentioned the plentiful display of autumn fruits she had seen on the journey. And Aunt Emily hoped this did not predict too severe a winter.

Louise brought in tea with some fresh scones and plum jam. Aunt Emily laughingly told Leah as a nursing mother to go lightly with the jam as it might upset the baby - according to an old wives' tale. Then she added that perhaps it was uncooked plums that should be avoided.

Leah's mother appeared more relaxed as they talked together. But soon, noticing the time, she grew anxious about getting home.

While Louise gave her a quick tour of her daughter's home, Aunt Emily told Leah that her father knew nothing of her mother's visit as he was attending an annual Church meeting. She would tell him on her return. And naturally, she was nervous about how he would react to her disclosure.

As Aunt Emily drove away with her sister, no mention was made of bringing her for any further visits. Leah had hoped for a meeting between her mother and Ray, but Aunt Emily said it was better not to involve her mother too much for the present.

The baby was christened in his father's church and given the names, Stephen Hugh, after Ray's brother and their paternal grandfather. Leah was pleased the child behaved so well on his first outing among his father's people, and wearing the family christening shawl.

A party was held at the bungalow for all immediate friends and relations, with Louise and Muriel helping with the catering. The baby was the centre of attention until Leah took him away finally - to be fed and hopefully put down to sleep for a few hours.

"Don't be lifting him every time he cries, or feeding him, either," Ray's cousin, Marie, advised on Leah's return. "You could spoil him and never have a minute's peace. Believe me - I know - I've been through this six times!"

"Well - I wouldn't let him cry for too long," Con's wife, Maureen, warned. "I've heard a baby boy can be ruptured easily."

By the end of the evening, Leah was feeling quite confused by all the conflicting advice she had been given. But in the days that followed, although she missed Aunt Emily's calming presence, she was soon beginning to cope with having a baby in the home.

There were nights of course, when she felt tired-out from getting up to change and feed her son. And when he cried bitterly she often didn't know what to do with him. Muriel brought her a soothing preparation from the chemist to give to him.

"It'll be useful when he's teething," she said. But now she advised Leah to walk about with the child over her shoulder or to rub his back and hope he had only a temporary pain from wind in his tummy.

Sometimes Ray woke up and took a turn at walking about with Stephen in his arms. But Leah soon sent him back to bed. She felt that Ray needed all the sleep he could get for dealing with his

113

heavy outside work.

Earlier in the year, Ray had enlarged his dairy herd to bring in bigger cheques from milk sales and to supply further calves for rearing. He was also housing more beef cattle. Ray now had to meet all the work and expense of keeping two homes going. He reminded Leah that life had also acquired a new purpose and meaning - now that he had a wife and child to provide for. He looked happy, too, Leah thought, as he hugged them both and waved goodbye each morning.

But Leah worried about Ray being out in all weathers. With the approach of another winter, her knowledge of farming had greatly increased. Some autumn ploughing had been done, but hedges had to be cut and mended, potatoes dug, turnips and carrots lifted, apples picked, a tree felled for winter fuel as well as all the general work.

Just lately, there had been days of heavy rain and leaves were blocking drains and gutters. The ground at gateways and other areas had become water-logged and muddy from constant movement of cattle. Ray's clothes were often damp and smelling of the farm-yard, especially when manure, carted to the fields and stacked there earlier in the year, was being spread on stubble land left from the grain harvest. Leah loved to see a fine windy day to dry the whole place as well as all the washing she had for her family.

As the days passed, baby Stephen had fewer wakeful nights and his daily routine of bathing, dressing, feeding, sleeping was beginning to follow a more settled pattern. Leah often carried him about the house showing him colourful things and talking to him. And when he smiled, she would hold him close marvelling at this amazing little person who had come to Ray and herself and was so mysteriously a part of them both.

She knew she was lucky to have more time with her child than many farmers' wives and even other mothers. Some afternoons, she wrapped him up warmly and wheeled him in his pram to his grandmother so that she herself could help Louise. There was packing and cleaning of eggs, fowl to feed and sometimes a few to be plucked for the local butcher. By early December, Louise had a splendid flock of over seventy turkeys as well as other fowl ready for the Christmas market.

Leah also kept Ray's farming records up to date: milk and beef production, sales of all their crops, the births and marketing of calves . . .

Her neat notes beside Ray's hurried jottings made him smile. Sometimes she wrote his business letters when he had little time. Watching Muriel tapping out even neater efforts on her new typewriter reminded Leah of her own efficient machine lying idle in the city. Had her father, she wondered, made sure it was kept, like herself, well out of sight. Aunt Emily had reported that he had left the room, refused to listen when her mother had tried to tell him of seeing Leah and her child.

Soon there was excitement everywhere with the Christmas festivities - friends calling, presents being exchanged. Ray's sisters, Eileen and Kathleen had arrived for a few days and on Christmas Eve the whole family attended midnight Mass. Leah assured Ray that she was quite happy sitting at home with the baby. It was on occasions like this, with the evidence of deep religious fervour going on around her, that she was especially conscious of the difference between her own beliefs and those held by Ray.

But, strangely, the strong attachment he had to his religion and all that it involved, gave her a sense of family stability, love and security - something her own home had finally failed to give her, in spite of guarding her from the ills of the world and what her father considered to be the most harmful influences.

Christmas Day was spent at the farmhouse where Louise and her mother had been busy for weeks with cooking and festive preparations. Among the seasonal decorations a lighted candle stood in a front window to welcome any lonely travellers. On a side table, Louise had set out a little crib for the Bethlehem scene.

"We have kept this miniature stable with Mary, Joseph and Baby Jesus from our childhood days," she told Leah. "We just re-arrange it each year with fresh straw and hay for the animals."

Leah was still somewhat in awe of Ray's visiting sisters in their Nuns' habits. But the presence of the baby drew even Kathleen into a shared happiness as each nursed him and carried him around. Leah could understand Kathleen's uncertainty about the effects of Ray's marriage on the family.

She thought of her own parents at this time, too. Once again, she

115

had sent them greetings but, as usual, no word had come from them. And Leah expected none; she understood only too well her mother's position. And she knew from Aunt Emily, before she left to see her daughter in England, that they were both in fairly good health.

In the dark, wintry days of the New Year, trees and hedges stood bare. Only the ivy on tree-trunks and walls and a few evergreen trees and bushes gave colour to the faded landscape. Leah loved the warm and friendly brightness of their log and turf fires. It made her feel safe when heavy white frost covered gardens, fields and roofs, crunching underfoot and glistening coldly in the moonlight. It also crept relentlessly across cold window-panes in unheated rooms.

Leah felt glad that the cattle were housed these days, although this brought extra work and expense to keep them clean, fed and watered.

The presence of her baby kept Leah from being lonely on the days she remained at home to do house-work or as she prepared the evening meal. She also listened to the radio. Sometimes, a lively tune would set her dancing, often with the baby in her arms.

Ray's favourite meal was a meat pie or a stew with dumplings, followed by baked rice with sultanas or stewed apples or plums with custard. When visitors were coming for supper, she did extra baking: perhaps sausage rolls and a fruit flan; salmon and mushroom pasties and a fruit cake. On the nights they went visiting, Louise stayed with Stephen, making sure she had a bottle of boiled water ready in case he woke up. Sometimes Ray's mother came too. But she was prone to attacks of bronchitis and did not go out on cold nights.

Gradually the weather changed to longer spells of sunshine, a few milder days. Soon Ray and Davy were ploughing and planting; the amazing cycle of growth had begun again. As always, it meant hard work on the farm with many disappointments regarding the weather. But this renewal of life throughout all of Nature seemed to affect everyone with a sense of hope and excitement for the days ahead.

Baby Stephen had acquired his first two teeth and the pupils of his eyes, which lately had shown mysterious tints of hazel, were now darkening to an all-over deeper brown. Ray's mother smiled

116

as she fondly watched her energetic grandchild jumping tirelessly on his father's knee. The baby was also trying out his voice production using a varied range of notes that surprised and delighted him.

During the winter months, Leah and Muriel had driven over occasionally to see each other. But one fine afternoon Leah decided to walk through the village with Stephen in his pram. First she called with Mrs Linton who always liked to see the baby. Now she told Leah that Jim had brought Lindy to see them and they had all got on very well.

"Maybe I've been a bit hard on Lindy. As you and Muriel told me, there's more to that young lady than just a love of dancing."

Leah said goodbye and walked on towards the village. As she approached the first cottage, the owner, a large, bossy-looking woman, was standing stiffly in the doorway looking out. Leah, as she passed, smiled a little nervously towards her. But in return received a stony stare.

Then the woman called after her: "So that's a wee Papish you're wheeling along there. May God forgive you! And no doubt there'll be more of the same before long."

Shocked and hurt, Leah hurried on, glad to see Lindy at the Post Office hurrying out to admire Stephen and his pram and then to tell her about Jim and their latest outings to the city dance-halls.

Leah went on her way, meeting two women she had known very well in the past. They now gave her cool, unsmiling nods. Once again, she felt deeply hurt and unhappy.

Muriel was very sympathetic, telling her there were always a few people about who are unable to accept certain new situations - especially the complicated one that she had got herself into. "You're trying to keep a foot in two religious camps, our church and Ray's! Nobody about here has ever attempted to do that. And now you're rearing a little Catholic son!"

"Well," Leah countered, "I believe that true Christianity can be found among the members of any church following God's teaching and commandments."

"And I agree," Muriel said. "True Christianity, they say, is in the heart and mind. But no matter how we try to be worthy, it's still very difficult in this life not to tread on someone's toes, from a religious point of view - or any other way." She made a woeful

117

face. "And don't I know it!"

Muriel's Robert was now running and falling about the yard and fields following his father. Her second child was due in a few months' time and she confessed she was often glad of her mother-in-law's help. She was kept busy with her egg-business; it was flourishing and had been extended. Tom was heavily into keeping beef cattle. Recently, they had bought a bigger car, new machinery . . . all with opposition from Mrs Coulter, senior.

Soon it was time for Leah to leave, and she was growing increasingly anxious about the return journey. As other visitors had now arrived she said nothing to Muriel of her sudden decision. But, away from the house, she turned on to a narrow road that ran well out into the country, rising later to pass the chapel on the hill and then a further hill before bringing her home in an opposite direction from the village.

It was a long and lonely journey of three or four miles, but Stephen had been fed and was sleeping peacefully. As she hurried on, glad not to be meeting anyone, she was getting into a nervous state worrying about the further unpleasantness she had suffered.

As Muriel's friend, the village people had welcomed her. They had always shown friendship to Ray. But it was clear her marriage to Ray had altered the situation for them both - with some people. And now the birth of their child had worsened matters considerably. Ray must have noticed this too, and the thought saddened her.

By the time Leah let herself into the bungalow, she was feeling both tired and despondent, and trying not to cry. She lifted Stephen from his pram, changed and fed him. Then she sat holding him to her as tears filled her eyes. What was she to do? Go away and bring no further trouble to Ray's family?

On an impulse, she got up quickly and began to wrap the child in a warm shawl, thinking rapidly. She would leave at once and take him with her. But, wide awake now, the child objected strongly to this treatment. He began to kick and cry bitterly. Leah, forced to unwrap him, placed him on the floor with his toys and he bashed away happily.

And Leah knew there was nowhere to go. Her aunt had let the room she once had. She had no other home anywhere, no means of support. Besides, the baby was Ray's too. The three of them

118

belonged together no matter what trouble might come their way.

Leah washed her face in cold water, tidied herself and began to make the evening meal. Muriel had said to ignore the hurtful things that some people might do or say. Lots of pleasant things had also happened that day. She and Ray had many good friends; she would remember that.

Ray looked tired when he arrived that evening. He smiled at Leah a little sadly before peeping at his now sleeping son. Then he held out his arms and drew her to him.

"Leah, Leah - you came home the long way from Muriel's today - pushing the pram up those steep rough hills. Louise saw you from the top field. I'm so sorry that you felt you had to do this."

"It was a mistake," Leah told him. "I know that now. It's not a good way to come home at all." She held him tightly.

"Good girl," he said. "I know it's tough. But we're both in this together and we're going to face it out."

Leah gave him a bright smile. "Come on, and we'll have our dinner while his lordship's still sleeping."

During the following weeks, Leah often wheeled Stephen into the village, though not without some anxious moments, especially passing the cottage. Some people avoided her, but she soon knew those who offered friendship.

By the summer, Stephen was crawling around everywhere, trying to empty exciting-looking cupboards and tearing up any books and papers within reach. Leah's emphatic "No!" and shaking of her head went unnoticed for some time, but gradually, he came to understand there were some things he must not do. At the same time, a certain light in his eyes showed he enjoyed the challenge of a try.

Aunt Emily came for Stephen's first birthday party and took several snaps with her Brownie camera. He wore the navy trousers and light blue jersey made and sent by Leah's mother, and the blue socks and patent shoes from Aunt Emily. Louise and his other Granny had bought him a warm, winter coat and pull-ups in dark maroon.

Stephen had almost mastered the art of balance so, from a safe position, he was encouraged by his young guests to step out on his own to reach his presents left temptingly at some distance. After a shaky step or two, he would drop to the floor and crawl rapidly to seize a new toy with squeals of delight. Ray's cousin, Lucy, had brought her two young children, Shane and Rose, and with Robert and the others Stephen had great fun. Then, after jelly, birthday cake, biscuits and orange drinks, Maureen's and Con's daughter, Orla, aged seven, walked Stephen round and round the front rose-bed until they both collapsed, tired out.

The following day, to Leah's great surprise, Stephen was moving about the house, walking with great assurance from one support to the next.

Muriel's daughter was born early in December and named Anne Elaine. "The 'Anne' is for Tom's mother - to keep her happy, and well worth it," Muriel reported. "Besides, she looks like her granny at the moment - the same tight little mouth and keen blue eyes."

Then it was Christmas again. But this year it passed a little quieter at the farmhouse as Ray's mother was confined to bed with a bronchial cold and her family were anxious about her. But Mrs Anderson was up again and feeling well for the New Year.

About this time, too, Leah was looking a little pale and experiencing some weariness. But her heart often beat faster from the knowledge that by the following summer, she and Ray might have their second child. And, if it should be a girl, would she have the courage, or be able, to carry out the plan she had kept in her heart for some time?

THIRTEEN

From the plantation on the hill beyond the house, Leah heard the rasping sound of a cross-cut saw followed by the crash of a tree. Further sawing and chopping would follow as Ray and Davy prepared logs for winter fires. At other times they might be mending gates and hedges, clearing drains and ditches and doing other necessary maintenance about the place. Wet days were sometimes spent in the big hay-shed overhauling machinery in preparation for the spring-time work. There were often friendly exchanges with neighbouring farmers: an offer of help, a loan of some equipment.

Up at the farmhouse, Louise and her mother had made apple cheese and chutney from some of the apples laid out on the floor of the barn-loft for use through the winter. All jars had been neatly labelled, some for Leah to take home, while the rest were added to their earlier stocks of jams and preserves.

More time could now be spent on knitting and needlework. Ray's mother who, in her younger days, had done intricate crochet work at the convent in County Kerry, was working on a lovely border of lace for a linen tablecloth for Leah and Ray. Leah, herself, was busy knitting with the supply of wool and patterns brought by Aunt Emily from sales in the city.

Helen and Sean, who had been married shortly after Leah and Ray, were expecting their second child in the spring. They often motored out at weekends with baby John to see Leah and Ray. Sean, a teacher in the city, was a farmer's son and interested in Ray's work. Leah and Helen had plenty to talk about. They often 'phoned each other to discus baby matters.

On Aunt Emily's last call with Leah's parents she had found her father ill with influenza and her mother just recovering. But she had left her looking happier on receiving the photographs of Leah and her son on his first birthday. She had looked a little frightened as she said: "I'll return these photos very soon; Matthew mustn't see them."

Winter passed slowly with cold dark days when rain and hail battered the windows like angry gravel and winds tortured the trees, roaring through the branches at night, reminding Leah of a storm at sea.

Sometimes, a roof-slate came crashing down from house or barn. There were also times when they were troubled with coughs and colds and then she made hot bedtime drinks from their plentiful supply of blackcurrant jam which usually brought more restful sleep.

'March came in like a lion and went out like a lamb'. Leah and Stephen walked round the fields behind the house where each day brought further opening of leaves and flowers. A spraying of delicate green gradually covered the dark winter trees and hedges. Woodland creatures began to stir from sheltered quarters to search for food.

Stephen would stand, brown eyes wide with wonder as he listened to and tried to mimic the sounds and movements around them. There was gurgling water chuckling musically in over-filled drains and ditches; birds in flight that cheeped and trilled about their business of building nests; new-born lambs bleating loudly as they frolicked on the hillside.

The whole countryside grew lush and green with growing crops; gardens bloomed afresh through days of sun and showers. Sometimes Leah called with Muriel's mother for a chat or motherly advice. Her own health was very good but it was reassuring to talk things over with someone as understanding as Mrs Linton. On one topic only did she show concern.

"I know you and Ray have been very happy together with your little son. But Muriel tells me that if you should have a daughter this time, you would like to rear her as a Protestant - to try to bring a little happiness to your parents. But is this wise, Leah? Surely it would divide you as a family?"

"Ray and I don't feel divided and we keep our own religious views. Many couples have different ideas and interests and - "

"I wasn't thinking of you and Ray, exactly," Mrs Linton

interrupted. She looked thoughtful but she said nothing more.

These days, when going to see Muriel, it was less tiring for Leah to take the car. She was also feeling a little self-conscious about meeting certain people in the village. Stephen loved to play with Muriel's two children and was happily unaware that Granny Coulter, when present, walked away on Leah's arrival. She felt thankful that it would be some time before Stephen sensed he was not a welcome guest to people like Mrs Coulter, senior, who had not spoken to Leah since her marriage.

Sometimes Leah worried that Stephen might blame his parents later on for placing him in the invidious position of not knowing where his allegiance lay in certain circumstances. For the present she decided to put these thoughts aside. She and Ray were becoming used to being received with a certain stiffness by some of his relations and former friends. But Louise worried about them.

"Oh, Leah - I do wish you were one of us - truly one of us. Then we could all be happy." She sighed and shook her head. "I know it just can't be. And it's all so sad."

Ray's mother went on her quiet way, saying little. But Leah guessed she must often suffer because of her son's marriage.

Leah liked the care-free sunny days when Muriel took them all in her big family car to do shopping in the local town. Afterwards, the children enjoyed the swings in the park before they had tea in their favourite cafe. Before going home, they called with Muriel's cousin, Christine, at their shop in the High Street. Here they stocked up with oranges, bananas and fresh fish. Sometimes Leah made kedgeree with fish, rice and hard boiled eggs, similar she hoped to a favourite dish of Ray's, made in the past by his mother.

On these visits to town, Leah bought several items for the coming baby. Again, everything was white with no trimmings of pink or blue. And she tried to keep her mind clear of any thoughts regarding the arrival of a son or daughter. But as the time drew near, it was impossible not to wonder and feel a little nervous about what she might have to do.

Then, towards the end of June, Patrick Raymond Anderson, their second son was born. As he was placed in her arms, she felt no disappointment. She even had a sense of relief, especially when she saw the pleasure of the Anderson family. It also meant that no decisions had to be taken or any changes made in their home life.

Yet thoughts of her unhappy father often came to trouble her. The only way she had any hope of bringing him some happiness might never come to pass. It could also come too late.

Only Ray understood the strange battle going on inside her. "No little girl - yet," he had said softly, embracing them both. Then, lifting the baby, tightly wrapped up, and holding him in one arm, he placed the other around Stephen. Leah smiled, knowing that whatever children God might send them that would be all right with Ray. He would accept each child as God's will and ask for His help to deal with any troublesome situations that might arise.

For Leah, the rearing of Patrick began with much greater confidence than during the first months with Stephen. Patrick was a quieter baby, perhaps sensing he was in experienced hands and so had little to shout about. The weather was kinder, too, and Leah was soon out walking with her two children.

For the present, she avoided the village; the place had been decorated for the recent Twelfth of July, the Protestant celebration of the Battle of the Boyne. Lines of flags and coloured bunting traversed the main street, Union Jacks still hung from many top windows and arrangements of orange-lilies looked out from parlours below.

Leah remembered it all from those earlier days when she had stayed with the Lintons. She and Muriel had joined the people on the street to enjoy the colourful spectacle and the music of Orange bands.

At times, Muriel had burst into song with verses from 'The Sash My Father Wore' and 'On the Green Grassy Slopes of the Boyne'. The Orangemen had come from around the country, flying their banners - sometimes King William on a white horse - as they walked on their way to the 'field' for the day's outing. And Mr Linton and Jim had been in the procession.

Ray had never joined them on these occasions; he had watched the procession from a field and waved as they passed. At that time Leah had not known of Ray's different religion and allegiances.

She also had had a very limited knowledge of her country's history and politics. Her father's bitterness towards Roman Catholics had seemed to her an entirely religious matter resulting from his own family feuds of the past.

Now she was beginning to realise that the acrimony between

many Protestants and Catholics went deeper than differences of religion. But surely such hostility could have little to do with Christianity? Thoughts that had puzzled her before were still very disturbing.

Even Muriel, trying to warn her of the difficulties of marrying into a Catholic family, had had little knowledge of the full undercurrent of enmity that existed between certain sections of the two communities. Ray had tried to explain about some of the differences between them.

"Your people, Leah, are Unionists and Protestants - wanting to maintain union with Britain. But not many would wish to resort to violence. My people are Nationalists and Catholic, hoping to re-unite Ireland. But most Nationalists are also against violence."

Leah still felt uneasy about the subjects of religion and politics, sensing something she did not really understand, and over which she and Ray could have no control.

Ray, watching her, said quickly: "Don't worry, Leah. Any outbursts of disagreement between the two factions soon blow over. There hasn't been any real trouble for some time." He smiled. "Even feelings in the village seem to be a little more tolerant lately. Nobody walked out of Nesbitt's shop without speaking when I went in yesterday."

Yes, Leah thought, Ray always looked on the bright side and kept her spirits up.

When baby Patrick was three months old and Stephen nearly three years, Leah's mother arrived again to see her. As before, it was Aunt Emily who suggested the visit, reminding her sister that Matthew appeared to be in better health lately. "Just tell him straight out that you want to see your daughter, and that you are most unhappy."

As Leah's father blamed Aunt Emily for helping Leah towards her disastrous marriage, he always left the room on her arrival. But the door was open and she heard her sister's quiet entreaty as she told him how she longed to see her daughter and grandchildren.

Matthew's reply had been gruff and impatient: "Go if you must, Margaret. But you go without my approval. And remember, I don't wish to hear anything more on the matter."

Aunt Emily 'phoned to say they were on their way and Leah watched for the car in a state of nervous anticipation. For now, at last, her mother and Ray would be meeting for the first time. And she hoped so much they would like each other.

She need not have worried. A short time later, she watched them chatting together, each fondly holding Stephen and Patrick in turn. Her mother's hair was almost white now, but there was a brightness about her, a softening of tension in the lines of her face as she sat there among them. Leah wondered how her father could bear to keep her so unhappy. Her mother always thought of him and, very soon, anxious not to upset him, she said she must be on her way home.

Their next visitors were Helen and Sean who arrived from the city with John and baby Aidan, two months younger than Patrick. While Ray and Sean walked round the fields, Leah and Helen with prams and children strolled along the country road.

Shortly after this, a new excitement was gripping the farmhouse. Ray's brother, Stephen, was expected home after his visit to Rome. He would then be returning to his work on the Missions in South America. His mother and Louise had been preparing for his coming for weeks. And Ray and Davy, once the harvest was in, had been painting the place inside and out.

Leah felt anxious about this meeting with Father Stephen. What would he really think about the wife his brother had chosen? He would know she was not conforming to the religion held to be so important by all the members of his family. He was probably worried about the future of his nephews in Leah's hands.

On the afternoon of his arrival, Leah was ready to take the children for a walk before calling at the farmhouse when Father Stephen suddenly appeared at the open door, dressed in his dark clerical garb. Not so tall as Ray, brownish hair cut shorter, eyes darkly solemn and questioning, Father Stephen, at that moment, had the distant look of his mother. For a moment, Leah stood feeling slightly intimidated. But when he smiled and shook hands, she was reminded of Ray's kindly manner and her tenseness relaxed.

"I have arrived home a little earlier than was expected," Father Stephen explained, with just a trace of a Southern Irish accent. "So I have been sent to bring you up to the house right away. They're preparing some tea for us. I'm told the big feast will be held tonight for all the visitors coming."

He turned to the children, peeping into the pram at the sleeping Patrick, then lifting Stephen and swinging him round to the child's great delight.

"So this young man is my namesake - and I see a strong, family likeness. I hope you are a good boy, Stephen."

As they all set off, Father Stephen put a hand to the pram and, while his young nephew danced along beside him, he began to reminisce about his own youthful days. "Ray was the baby. I often had the job of minding him, especially when we were working in the fields and he kept following us." He stopped for a few moments, gazing about him with a look of appreciation. "And now - he's the one doing all the work to keep this place in such great order."

They found Louise singing in the kitchen, a tea-pot in her hand. Her mother, turning from the window where she had watched their approach, looked flushed and happy.

When Ray came in, having washed and tidied himself, they all sat down for tea with sandwiches and cakes. Afterwards, the two men went off together. Their mother took the children for a walk and Leah and Louise made final preparations for the evening entertainment.

Appetising smells were soon wafting through the house as the cooking continued: vegetable soup, roast beef, roast chicken, apple tarts and fancy cakes. Visitors began to arrive and Father Stephen was given a great welcome.

Most of Ray's relations had a smile for Leah. Those who were less friendly no longer worried her so much. She felt she understood their feelings about her much better now.

There was great excitement later on as everyone, proud of Father Stephen's achievements, sat listening as he spoke about his work abroad among so many of the world's poorest people. He also told them of his stay in Rome, of the crowds of pilgrims, Saint Peter's with the beautiful paintings and sculptures and the wonderful Michelangelo dome.

Ray smiled at Leah with a contented look, recognising that she, too, was interested and happy. These days, with her greater knowledge of Ray's cultural past, she could recognise the appeal and the significance of certain aspects of his beliefs. She now joined those making comments and asking questions, no longer feeling such an outsider as in the early days of her marriage.

When Father Stephen had done much visiting and left again, Ray told Leah of talks they had had. "I told him you were grieving about your parents, that you longed to see them happier. And that if we should have a daughter, you would like to bring her up in the Protestant Faith, and so, perhaps, dispel some of the gloom in their lives. I think Stephen understands. But, of course, he wishes it could be otherwise."

Ray smiled apologetically, and Leah felt that, in his heart, Ray must wish likewise. But she knew it would make no difference to his loving acceptance of a daughter. Just as she loved her sons, no matter what church they attended. Leah only hoped they would grow up to be good Christians. That was all that really mattered.

Another winter went by, often beautiful in its harshness and busier than ever for Leah with two children, often noisily active, and sometimes a cause for worry when laid low with childhood ailments.

Then, when spring was at its brightest, with spells of warm sunshine and sudden showers, Leah knew her third child was on the way. And this time, as the days passed, her early indisposition continued right through the summer and into the autumn.

"You're tired," everyone said, "with two active little boys."

"I bet you'll have a girl this time," Muriel told her. "They often give the most trouble - even at this early stage."

But Leah again refused to give much thought to this possibility. The doctor told her to rest as much as possible, but that was often quite difficult to do. There were days when, feeling ill and utterly weary, she watched Ray going off with his mother and sister for yet another attendance at their church or some other call on his time.

But soon her feelings of resentment would vanish. She knew that Ray wished to show his people that marriage to Leah had not greatly upset the family way of life. He was equally anxious not to neglect Leah.

Always, they readily forgave each other over any disagreement. It was important to them both to remain the best of friends, and for neither of them to regret their marriage. Muriel and Tom often had heated arguments over things like money and family problems. But Leah and Ray tried to settle any difficulties in a more understanding way.

128

It was early in December when Leah went into hospital. The following day, she and Ray were smiling over their dainty, fair-haired daughter, weighing seven pounds and looking perfectly healthy. She was a joy to them both and, for the present, they had no thoughts beyond these happy moments.

Leah, still rather pale and weak, was kept in hospital a few days extra. But she was recovering rapidly and felt spoiled by all the friends and relations who came to see her and brought flowers and other gifts. Even Ray's mother, in her quiet way, welcomed the new arrival. But sometimes Leah thought she saw a sadness in her dark eyes as they rested on her little grand-daughter; unlike the boys, she knew this child, like Leah, could never be quite one of the family.

Shortly after arriving home, Leah and Ray agreed to name the baby, Margaret Ruth, after Leah's mother and the child's paternal grandmother. She would be known as Ruth, they decided. And, with Muriel and Tom as godparents, she was baptised in the village church. Aunt Emily took photographs of the occasion and gave them, together with the baby's baptismal certificate, to Leah's mother.

"I told Margaret," Aunt Emily said, "to leave everything lying open where Matthew could see that his grand-daughter was now a member of a church similar to where his mother had belonged. And when Ruth is a little older, with Ray's and your mother's consent, I think it might be a good idea for me to take Ruth to see them." She smiled at Leah.

"Is this what you would like to happen?"

Leah could only nod; her aunt's kindness overcame her; she seemed to know all that was in Leah's heart regarding her parents and what she hoped to do for them.

PART 2

FOURTEEN

Leah stood with Ray in the front garden of the farmhouse looking down towards the road and watching Aunt Emily in her little green car driving off with their daughter. As she turned towards the city she raised a hand in farewell. Aunt Emily had changed very little in the past few years except that her hair was whiter, her face a little thinner. Beside her, in a pretty blue dress, fair curls tied in a pony-tail with a matching blue ribbon, sat five-year-old Ruth waving vigorously and looking delighted about this outing.

"It's wonderful, isn't it," Leah remarked, as they disappeared from view, "how Ruth never tires of going to see her grandparents? And Aunt Emily says they can't wait to see her; they're watching at the window every time. They have been different people since Ruth came into their lives. Now that she's older and off school for the summer, they'd like to have her for a few days instead of a few hours. Aunt Emily would stay with them, too; she wouldn't mind; my father treats her less coolly these days. After leaving Ruth there, she usually goes shopping or calls with friends. When she comes back, Mother and Ruth have a lovely tea ready for them all." Leah spoke brightly, refusing to dwell on less pleasant events that had also taken place and left her deeply disappointed.

As she turned with Ray towards the house, she felt the heat of the sun as she breathed in deeply the rich summer scents of the garden and looked about her at the growing crops, the lush greenery of the countryside.

A light breeze stirred her flowered skirt and tossed her hair, cut shorter these days. And her wide blue eyes continued smiling with the happy light of achievement. But when she glanced at Ray, her expression changed.

He had put on a little weight lately but it suited his height and

131

broad shoulders and added to his strong, healthy appearance. She thought of his continued love and care for herself and the children, his patient manner with everyone. But just now she had caught a suspicion of strain in those kindly, dark eyes. Was he trying to look pleased for her sake?

"Oh, darling, I'm sorry," she said. "There can't be much satisfaction for you in all this talk about Ruth. And here I am - keeping on about it."

"Leah, I am happy only when you are happy. Surely you know that? We both knew it would be necessary to accept certain conditions in our life together. Rearing Ruth as a Protestant has given your parents a new interest in life and some peace of mind for you. Our arrangement hasn't worked out too badly at all. And I think most people about here have got used to us now."

Leah smiled as he took her hand. Yes, life had been busy for them both, but with few really serious problems. Stephen, Patrick and Ruth loved the village school and all their young friends. And she and Ray enjoyed chatting with other parents as they watched their children performing together at school sports, summer fetes, the yearly concert.

"Come in for a cup of tea," she said. "You could do with a rest. Then you can take some to Davy up in the hay field."

A car horn sounded on the road and they waved to Lindy and Jim, married this past four years and out with their two-year-old twin daughters.

A faint smell of paint met them as they passed through the porch and hall into the big kitchen. The farmhouse had been completely redecorated and most of their own furniture now stood in some of the rooms alongside several pieces left by Ray's mother when she and Louise had moved to the bungalow.

The idea of changing houses had been suggested by Ray's mother some months earlier. "It's the sensible thing to do," she told Ray. "You and Leah need more room with your growing children. And the time has come when I feel like retiring from the centre of things." Her eyes had clouded a little as she added: "Besides, the bungalow is where your father and I had planned to live - when the right time came. And, for me, that time is now."

It had been a big upheaval for all of them, but finally they had seen to everything and settled in. Louise had had her hens and their

132

houses moved to the field behind the bungalow. Leah had since been rearing pullets so that she would have laying fowl of their own. With Louise coming often to work with her in the large back garden, their flowers, vegetables and fruit were as plentiful as ever. Leah knew that Ray was pleased to be back in his old home and so she felt happy there too.

Friends and relations called more often than usual to see how both families were getting along. They seemed greatly interested at the change-over of houses. Muriel, coming with Robert, Anne and her youngest, Joan, kept telling Leah how lucky they were to have such a fine place all to themselves. Leah knew that Muriel and Tom were not too badly off with their own living arrangements. But Muriel could never forget her involvement in bringing Leah and Ray together, and it pleased her to think that life was going well for them.

Muriel had certainly eased their return into the village community with her cheery, see-no-difficulty manner. The occasional outbreak of trouble between Catholics and Protestants in other places distressed Leah but seemed to be little worse than it had ever been. Helen and Sean, arriving with their family, mentioned one or two rather disturbing incidents that had occurred in the city. Their children, John, Aidan and little Kate, appeared to be free of any worries as, shouting and laughing, they raced about exploring out-buildings and fields with Stephen, Patrick and Ruth.

That summer of 1968 remained gloriously dry and sunny for long periods. As usual, Leah and Muriel took the children to the seaside in whichever family car was available. Leah loved to revisit places along the East coast where she and Ray had wandered so happily in their early days together. They always called with Aunt Emily and sometimes met Leah's cousin, Jane, and her family. Her eldest boy, Adam, whom Leah had bathed as a baby, would soon be doing his Qualifying Examination.

Other journeys were made travelling North to the children's favourite place, the Giant's Causeway. Here, with voices raised in excitement, they climbed among the fluted, hexagonal shapes to find the highest seats for themselves. It was fun trying to identify some of the strange formations: the Wishing Chair, the Giant's Horseshoe, the Organ, the Lady's Fan . . . Stephen and Robert were more venturesome than the girls or Patrick. Anne was busy keeping an eye to the safety of Ruth and her sister, Joan, reminding Leah of Muriel's motherly attention when they themselves were schoolgirls.

Further along the coast they liked to stop to bathe and then enjoy the contents of their picnic baskets. To Leah, these were wonderful and carefree days. While the children played on a lovely stretch of sand, she and Muriel rested, listening to the lazy splash of waves, a lulling background to the excited calls of happy young voices.

There were other happy days when Ray was not too busy and they went on family outings. Sometimes he took the boys to Gaelic football matches, meeting up with Con and his three lads. At other times they joined Tom and Robert for fishing expeditions in the Muldare river, while the girls played 'housie' in the Anderson garden. Later in the evening, Leah and Muriel called everyone to the big kitchen to enjoy a meal of fried trout and tomatoes with fresh griddle-bread and home-made butter.

Leah's children also had little tea-parties with Granny Anderson at their old home. The bungalow looked different and yet familiar as they re-examined the rooms. Sometimes, when Ruth was helping her Aunt Louise to gather and pack eggs, Ray's mother would put the boys over their Catechism. She was greatly pleased when each had taken his First Communion and Stephen had become an altar boy.

Louise had her own car now and, when the children were at school and Ray at cattle sales or other business, Leah often joined Louise and her mother on outings to friends and relations. Over the years, she had been made to feel more welcome. Even Ray's cousin, Judith, home at holiday times, seemed, more or less, to have accepted her.

Then, as the harvest ripened and everyone was busy, the news on radio and television told of increasing unrest among sections of the community, mostly of Ray's religion. They were marching in growing numbers to demand, among other things, fairer allocation of jobs and housing and One Man One Vote in local Government elections.

All this was leading to clashes with authority and people were being injured. Leah could see how Ray deplored these disturbing incidents, yet he felt that, in many instances, the grievances were well-founded.

Soon further demands were being made, reviving the old cause of enmity between Republicans and Unionists - the existence of a border between Northern Ireland and the Republic of Ireland.

Associations for peace were being quickly formed, talks given, all to try to heal the political differences of the Catholic and Protestant peoples.

Leah, like so many others, could only wait and hope that something could and would be done to ease the discontent and the storm that seemed to be gathering. People like the Andersons and the Lintons had no special grievances of their own to complain of. There were many others who felt a great need for social justice; they were far from satisfied with any of the proposed reforms.

As time went on further marches were taking place, the disturbing incidents continued, and were shown to the world on television. In the city of Derry, barricades were raised against authority and many people were badly injured in the resulting clashes. In certain areas of Belfast, stones and petrol bombs were being thrown into people's homes, and families were fleeing in terror. An uneasy feeling lay over both communities.

When the army was called in, a tall barrier, called 'The Peace Line', was erected between the two waring sections. Throughout the country most Catholics and Protestants were shocked and frightened at what was happening. And now Leah sometimes felt a subtle constraint in the company of members of either community.

At first she tried to keep the worst of the news from the children. But often at school they heard alarming stories of the happenings in many parts of the country. When two young boys arrived to stay in the village from a troubled area of the city, they frightened the school-children with their first-hand accounts of violence and the burning of people's homes.

"They shook their fists, Daddy," a wide-eyed Patrick retorted. "And they shouted about all the terrible things they would do to the enemies on the other side of the Peace Line."

"They used very bad language," Stephen put in.

"Who are these boys?" Leah asked.

"They've been sent here," Stephen explained, "to be safe from all the rioting in the streets at home. They're staying with their granny, that big woman in the first house who stares at us and mutters when she sees us passing."

Leah remembered the incident with the same woman after

Stephen was born. It had not been repeated to the same extent but Leah always felt anxious when passing her house.

"I'm glad we don't live in Belfast," Patrick said. "Will John and Aidan have to leave home, too?"

"Oh, I don't think so," Ray told him, trying to reassure the children. "But there *is* trouble in some parts of the country between certain sections of Catholics and Protestants."

Stephen stared at his mother in some puzzlement. "But you're a Protestant, aren't you, Mummy?"

"Oh, that doesn't matter," Leah said quickly. "We're all friends together around here - you know that. We don't worry about people's religion." In her heart she prayed it would always be so.

She was quite unprepared the following day when her two sons raced in from school, breathless and frightened.

"Those two boys from the city have been calling us funny names," Stephen said, panting.

"Yes," a red-faced Patrick put in, "and they kept pushing us out of the games in the playground today."

"And calling us dirty Fenians!" Stephen said, indignantly. "Then, just now, coming home, they ran past us down the hill, shouting: 'Hurry, hurry! The Fenians are after us!'" Stephen furrowed his brow. "Who are these Fenians, Mummy? Sure we're not Fenians?"

It was only a childish incident, but Leah had a moment of heart-stabbing alarm. "Of course not," she assured them. "Those boys don't know what they are talking about. You don't need to pay any attention to them."

She wasn't sure herself what Fenians were until Ray tried to explain that the name came from other troubled times in the country's history. An organisation, known as the Fenians, was formed in 1858 to draw attention to injustices by the use of force. They also pledged to work for complete severance from Great Britain. The society was eventually suppressed but its ideals lived on.

Ray took the occurrence with the city boys quite seriously and told Stephen and Patrick to say nothing that could cause any further unpleasantness. He promised to call for them the following day and speak to their teacher.

When his boys were again subjected to harsh treatment in the playground with several other children joining in, Ray arranged at once to send them to a Catholic school in the town. "They would be leaving soon, anyway," he said. "Just as I had to do. But, certainly, I did not have to leave because of something like this."

Ruth, in the Infants department and coming home earlier, had not been aware at first of her brothers' distress or of the way Leah's heart had raced anxiously during these discussions.

"You're all right," Patrick told his sister somewhat enviously, realising she would not have to make this sudden change of school. "You're different; you're a Protestant, like everyone else in the village. Those boys won't get at you."

Leah fervently hoped this would be so, but she knew she could not be sure of anything in the changing atmosphere around them. She continued to accompany Ray and the boys to their church on Sunday mornings, joining in with those parts of the service that seemed to her to be universal Christian practice and thanksgiving - with now added prayers for peace throughout the land.

As the rioting and violence continued in many places, Leah became increasingly aware of receiving fewer friendly looks and comments from the congregation around her. How could she blame them? While they held strong allegiance to their church and its members in these troubled times, they must wonder about her own loyalty. They knew she was sending her daughter Ruth to Sunday school and church with the Linton children. And she herself sometimes attended the evening service in the village church, where again several people glanced at her with disapproval.

Ray appeared to be less concerned about people's attitude to their family arrangements than she was. But she knew it was bound to trouble him at times.

"You'll find," he said, consolingly, "that our real friends understand and trust us. We must remember that."

He was right, Leah thought. But she certainly felt happier for Ruth when the two city boys had been sent away because their grandmother could no longer control them. In her heart, Leah felt a real understanding of how this present bitterness could divide the country.

And matters were growing worse - with increased rioting, shootings and buildings being bombed. Soon many members of the paramilitaries were being arrested. Some were charged and others were interned without trial. Further violence followed on both sides and in one horrific explosion in a Belfast bar, fifteen people died. Another terrible day of death occurred in Derry and became known as 'Bloody Sunday'. Some weeks later, an unbelievable bombing took place at a Belfast restaurant where two women died and over a hundred people were injured, many of them suffering severe mutilation.

Leah wondered what had happened to their beautiful country to bring such tragedy to its people. How could that old, bitter enmity between the two communities have been revived to the terrible extent of such warfare and suffering?

FIFTEEN

As Stephen and Patrick set off daily by bus for the town, Leah, like so many mothers, prayed for their safety. They attended the Christian Brothers School and both had passed their Qualifying examination. She watched proudly as they waved goodbye, dressed in their school uniforms, both slightly built, dark-eyed and dark-haired. During the past years they had made many friends among boys who joined the bus along the way, some going to the same school, while others, like Robert Coulter, were pupils at the Protestant grammar school. Only one or two from this school showed a lack of friendliness to Stephen and Patrick.

Leah's two boys were quite different in nature and ability. Stephen, quiet and thoughtful, was a real scholar, but he was always ready to help on the farm when he was needed. Already, he was looking forward to attending the University to continue his studying. He showed a great flair for languages, including Irish, which pleased his Granny Anderson - herself a fluent Irish speaker in her younger days. But she did not always agree with the teaching Stephen was getting at school. He tried to assure her there were variations in the language from place to place and, as he pointed out, she had learned to speak Gaelic in County Kerry.

Patrick, quiet in a different way, just managed to scrape through his exams. He liked more than anything to be out in the fields helping his father and Davy. Sometimes, he accompanied Davy when he went shooting rabbits and pigeons. He had learned that there was a need for this to save some of their crops. Soon he was pleased to be bringing home food for the family, already skinned or plucked and ready for Leah to cook.

Patrick also spent time with his hero, Robert Coulter, often joining him at his Grandfather Linton's place where Leah saw them climbing trees, helping Jim with cattle and sometimes fishing in the river below the house. Robert had grown into a strong-looking lad of medium height with a mass of unruly brown hair. Muriel had reported that now, at the age of fifteen, Robert was a great judge of cattle at the Y.F.C. competitions - and a very shrewd bargainer at cattle sales.

Despite the widespread troubles, life went on with little disruption around the village itself. But there was pain and disbelief on many faces as further atrocities were reported, often involving someone known to local people.

Leah and Ray still exchanged visits with relations and friends in the country, and spent evenings with Muriel and Tom, often at the Lintons' place. Lindy and Jim were usually present, still full of fun and trying to enjoy life between the dispiriting reports of further tragic happenings.

As Muriel said, her mother might not like Lindy's choice of wallpaper, her wild squeals of enthusiasm or protest as she went about her work, or her brief and fashionable skirts when she dressed to go out. She just remembered that Lindy was a splendid mother to her twin girls and baby son, and that she helped in the house and fields with equal readiness and showed no bias of friendship anywhere.

Occasionally they all went dancing, meeting their Farmers' Union friends in the town, trying to forget the state of their country and that fresh trouble could break out at any time, anywhere. Louise kept an eye on the children when Leah and Ray were absent. They themselves often sat with Ray's mother in the bungalow when Louise was out, sometimes with her friend, Dermot Hagan, one of the boys' teachers who often brought them home as he lived on a farm nearby.

Leah thought about those responsible for the bombing of homes, the killing and maiming often of innocent people and the terrible suffering being caused. She considered that this ruthless taking of life was a sin and wondered how men could bring themselves to do such cruel and ungodly acts.

Ray remembered young men he had met at the University, during his short time there, who had been caught up in the long-standing ideal of 'Ireland for the Irish', driven on by the seemingly glorious thought that they were helping to liberate their country.

140

Many, on both sides of the present fighting, Ray insisted, had not realised into what situations of horror they could be drawn. And their own deaths, their wounded bodies, even their imprisonment brought nothing but despair for their families, left to mourn wasted lives.

Most summers Leah and Ray managed to take the children for a few days' holiday to their favourite places on the west coast where it seemed their country's troubles could never reach. They loved the acrid smell of smoke from turf fires in wayside cottages fronted by fuchsia bushes and old-time scented roses, or as it drifted along village streets as they drove by.

They liked to watch the friendly donkeys on heathery slopes who came trotting down hopefully to view any parked car. The boldest would put woolly heads with eager mouths to open windows for a gift of biscuits or other titbits, and keep on asking for more. The wild goats kept their distance - often following their leader in single file along some precipitous path high on a mountain.

Always, there was the excitement of the sea in all its moods: the roaring turbulence of a storm with sea-birds crying; gentle sun-lit waves calling out the fishing boats from harbour and the bathers from the sweeps of golden sand.

In their hotel a few guests sometimes showed interest on hearing the Andersons came from the North of the country. Others appeared reluctant to talk on the subject. Many had ceased even to read or watch any of the news about the 'Troubles' of Northern Ireland.

"How do you live up there at all?" they were frequently asked. "We would be terrified to go near the place." Leah tried to explain that around their home and many other areas, there had been little disruption so far, and life went on normally.

One woman, on holiday with her daughter, sat listening, her face quite expressionless, her eyes dull.

Later, as she sat alone, she spoke to Leah. "Not so long ago," she said, "my son was attending the University in Belfast. Now he is interned for his part among those marching for better rights and conditions for so many people in need." She shook her head and looked sadly puzzled. "You see," she went on, "he was always a good, quiet lad, never hurtful or unkind. He just believed he was helping in a good cause for the betterment of our people. He never thought it would all turn into a cruel war."

141

She sighed. "At least I have one consolation: I know he can't be involved in the present blood-shed and destruction going on today. And I think he is sensible enough not to make trouble where he is."

In the months that followed, Leah often remembered that sad-faced woman. She hoped that the many conferences being held at high levels might soon settle the country's terrible unrest. But, as time went on, nothing really helpful was taking place; agreement between political members seemed difficult to reach. So the killing and destruction continued, bringing agony and despair to many more families.

Further trouble seemed on the way when a strike of electric-power workers closed many factories, crippling the country's industries and causing widespread distress, especially for the very young and the elderly. Leah and Ray, like many farmers, were now dependent on electricity for milking machines, freezers, poultry-rearing . . . And the cutting-off of supply brought loss and inconvenience. The strike was called off some days later when the power-sharing government resigned.

The best news people had had for a long time came just before the following Christmas, when a cease-fire was announced. Tensions eased like magic and Leah, shopping happily in town, saw strangers on the street nodding and smiling to each other, regardless of religious or political persuasions.

But all too soon, the following spring saw a continuation of death and destruction by both sides of the community. Leah and Ray grew anxious for the safety of their boys. Stephen was working hard for his G.C.E. examination at 'A' level, and Patrick as usual was doing as little study as possible. He and Robert liked to be free for the outdoor life they enjoyed so much. Leah felt they were trying to forget the horrors being enacted not so far away.

While people prayed daily at home and in every church for an end to the Troubles, Catholics and Protestants were coming together in a joint effort to try to heal the divisions between them. Leah and Muriel attended some of these meetings held in peoples' homes and local halls - to pray for greater friendship and understanding among them.

Certainly, after sensible discussions, everyone appeared to leave the meetings happier and more hopeful for the future. Leah met two people who, like Ray and herself, had entered into a 'mixed marriage'. They had recently left their new home and were trying to hide away, after being harassed and intimidated by neighbours and ostracised by their own families. Their windows had been smashed and an attempt made to set fire to their house.

"It's terrible to feel you are not wanted anywhere," the young wife said. "Coming to these meetings has made a great difference to both of us; it's great to feel you have friends again."

Leah had felt an ache of remembrance welling inside her. Yet always she and Ray had had many good friends to stand by them.

When Ray and Tom came along to one or two of these meetings, Tom said that this getting together appeared to be most encouraging for spreading goodwill and friendship. They discussed it later over supper together.

Ray looked thoughtful. "I have a feeling," he said, "that at these gatherings we are meeting mainly the kind of people from both communities who would always be friendly anyway. We all recognise a kindred spirit among us that has nothing to do with religion or politics. And that is why we can come together so easily and are so ready to shake hands." He gave them his usual slow smile. "But it is very comforting to find there are so many of us who think this way."

Leah and Muriel nodded in agreement. Ray, looking somewhat apologetic, glanced at Tom. "I think you would agree, Tom, that someone like your mother could never be persuaded to join us at these meetings."

Tom raised his eyebrows. "You're right, there; 'never' is the word."

"For that matter," Ray continued, "I don't believe my own mother would quite approve of what we're doing. But she does try to understand the different points of view of our two communities."

Yes, Leah thought, Ray's mother had always shown her kindness, but she must have found it difficult to accept her son's wife into the family. Leah's own father had preferred to banish his daughter rather than acknowledge Ray as his son-in-law. But he had accepted their daughter.

Leah knew she had Aunt Emily to thank for bringing this about. On her visits to Leah's parents, her aunt had brought photos of Ruth at various ages, and left them with her sister. Leah's mother had looked at them openly and finally placed them in a side-board drawer with all the others and the child's Baptismal Certificate. When she found on several occasions that their arrangement had been disturbed, she knew that Matthew had been looking at them.

Ruth had been about three years old at this time. And when Aunt Emily told Leah and Ray what had happened, she suggested that perhaps Ruth could now be taken to see her grandparents.

So, one summer day, she had surprised her sister by handing in the child, saying she would be back for her when her shopping was done. She knew that Ruth was a friendly little girl and had seen this other granny quite recently on one of her rare visits to the farm.

All the same, Aunt Emily had returned fairly promptly. And immediately she had sensed a different atmosphere in the house. But where was Ruth? She had looked around anxiously. Then her sister, with an excited gesture, had pointed through a back window to where Leah's father was walking hand in hand with his little grand-daughter, his head bent towards her as they chatted together.

Leah's eyes had filled with tears on hearing of this. For it meant that what she had planned and hoped for over the years had actually happened. Then a great longing came to her that she, too, might be friends with her father. Perhaps, after all this time, he would be ready to overlook the past and welcome her home? Surely this was now a real possibility.

Ray had not been so hopeful. "Your father's acceptance of Ruth doesn't mean he has changed in any way. I'm afraid his old hostility to Roman Catholics is still the same. In your father's eyes, Leah, you have joined the enemy."

But Leah had clung to the thought that, as people grow older, many seem to mellow in their attitudes to the beliefs and convictions they once held so strongly.

"Not your father!" Aunt Emily said, when Leah told her what was in her mind. "Look how he has ignored your poor mother's pleas all these years, when she begged him to recognise your existence. She still has to go against his wishes to see you occasionally, herself. I know how you must feel, Leah. But your parents are quite happy now with Ruth - and I think you should leave it like that."

Leah decided that perhaps Ray and her aunt were right to discourage her from presenting herself at her old home. Her father might shut himself away and refuse to see her. But she had another idea: she would join her parents at their place of worship. Surely there her father must at least acknowledge her? And, for the moment, that was all she would ask.

Leah would always remember that Sunday when she had asked Ray to drive her to the little hall with the plain glass windows and brick walls. Aunt Emily had finally been persuaded to warn Leah's parents of their daughter's intention to see them there.

Leah had dressed with care in a blue summer suit and navy straw hat with a turned-up brim - for blue had been the colour favoured for her by her father when she was young.

Sitting in the car, she had waited until most people had entered the building. Then, heart thumping, she had said goodbye to Ray, knowing he would watch anxiously until she reappeared.

As Leah slipped quietly on to the long seat beside her mother, where she had sat so often as a child, she felt nervously excited. Her mother's brief, anxious smile, from under her neat brown hat, was not greatly encouraging. Her father stared straight ahead. She glanced quickly at his stern profile, scarcely recognising him, shocked at how old he had grown, how thin and frail he looked.

As the congregation knelt in prayer or rose to sing, Leah tried to keep her mind on the order of the service. Once her mother moved an open book towards her and she tried to join in the singing, but her voice had such an uncontrollable tremor she had to stop.

It was a relief, later, when someone rose to speak and she could sit quietly listening. The small, grey-haired man soon caught her attention as he told a story involving the showing of mercy and forgiveness to one who had done wrong. He quoted from the Bible:

'Blessed are the merciful: for they shall obtain mercy.'

'Blessed are the peacemakers: for they shall be called the children of God.'

Leah glanced at her father. What was he thinking at this very moment, she wondered? He must have been listening, too. Surely his heart would be softening towards her? She had gone against his teaching - but that was all. And surely her punishment had been enough?

She did not know the hymn that had followed, but towards the end, the words rang out with relevance to the great problems of the moment. And her mother's gentle voice beside her gave added strength to their hopeful message:

'The stormy clangour of wild war-music -
O'er the earth shall cease.
Love shall tread out the baleful fire of anger,
And in its ashes plant the tree of peace.'

Leah's spirits rose; her whole body trembled in anticipation. She began dreaming of a complete reunion with her father - perhaps even a coming together with her husband and children.

When the congregation began moving from the seats, she followed, stepping aside in the aisle while her mother handed her father his stick and then held his arm. Leah waited expectantly, holding her breath and watching them. But her father's pale blue eyes never once sought her own imploring gaze.

Deeply hurt and disappointed, weighed down with sadness, she was also conscious of a great feeling of pity - for the pain in the drooping lines of her father's face, the weariness in the sagging shoulders under his grey Sunday suit.

She sighed deeply as she followed her parents' slow progress to the door. And now her heart was crying: how can my father treat me like this and continue to read his Bible day after day? How can he believe he is living the life of a true Christian?

They were the last to leave the building. Outside, sunlight patterned the path to the gate; a startled blackbird flew squawking from a tree and, out on the road, cars started up and began moving away. Only two remained, the neighbour, waiting for her parents; and Ray, to take her home.

Leah saw that her father had suddenly moved aside from her mother and was standing alone, both hands firmly on his stick as he stared away from them at distant buildings. Leah's mother regarded her sadly and shook her head. Leah knew then that this was her father's final dismissal telling her to go on her way, the way she had chosen. Holding back her tears, she pressed her mother's hand and hurried towards the gate.

In the years that followed, it had not been easy to forget that unhappy day. But when the Troubles came to their country with increased bitterness and enmity between her father's people and Ray's, Leah was grateful that her parents' happy relationship with their grand-daughter, Ruth, had not suffered in any way. At least she had tried for a reconciliation with her father. But she knew now she would probably never see him again.

SIXTEEN

Ruth was now seeing her grandparents more often than ever. Since passing her Qualifying Exam, she had been attending Leah's old school in the city, travelling by the bus that passed her home each morning.

Sometimes she stayed overnight with her grandparents - when school functions kept her late or they were anxious because some further trouble had been reported. Earlier in the year, indiscriminate shooting and bombing had taken place out in the country. Buses had been attacked causing the deaths of innocent people from both religious groups.

Aunt Emily had prevailed on her sister to have a 'phone installed now they were getting older, and this meant that Ruth was able to let her parents know when she expected to be home. But this was always done quietly without her grandfather's knowledge.

Ruth had set her heart on becoming a teacher, and this idea had the full approval of Leah and Ray. She was a light-hearted girl, full of fun and good-nature, who made friends easily. She considered that her position in a two-religion family was a very special one and gave her a great advantage over those she called 'just ordinary people', who could never have the same understanding or appreciation of the life-style of the so-called 'other side'.

From early days Ruth had learned the subjects to avoid when in her grandparents' house, having been well-instructed by Leah's mother.

"Poor old Grandad has a bee in his bonnet about people who go to Daddy's church. And I mustn't mention my brothers, either. For Grandad, they just don't exist. And of course, Mummy, I must never speak of you!"

At moments like this Leah would feel a knot of pain inside her -

pain for all the useless bitterness that was not only separating her from her father but was dividing the whole country.

"But Grandad is always ready to hear about my school-friends and the work we're doing. He's very strict, isn't he, about certain books that one should not read? I'm afraid I can't always tell him our full school programme. He's very interested in everything to do with church and Sunday school, and gives me Bible tracts with verses for daily reading. And he's delighted when I'm there to attend their own little church. Isn't he a strange, mixed-up old man? I feel so sorry for him, Mother."

Yes, Leah thought, that was the way she should take her father's rejection of herself - she should feel sorry for him. And she was thankful that she had her daughter to keep her in touch with her old home.

Ruth had friends everywhere. At home, there were the younger members of Ray's relations, and the Coulter children - especially Anne who hoped to become a nurse - and others they met at church functions and the village tennis courts. She also saw Helen's family, both in the city and at home, for they loved to have a day in the country.

It was they who brought the shocking news of the deaths of three young children in the city, killed by a gunman's car under fire from troops. This terrible tragedy led to women from both communities coming together in a vast movement for peace, called the 'Peace People'. Thousands from town and country, appalled and sickened by this latest killing and deeply saddened for the distraught family, gathered at a huge rally.

Charismatic and other Christian Revival meetings were also taking place, all hopeful of bringing to an end the death and destruction around them.

That summer Stephen passed his final school exams with excellent results, and Leah and Ray saw the strong possibility of their elder son considering a career away from farming. When they spoke to him about this, he said he had not quite decided what he would like to do. But he did know he was looking forward to reading English Literature and Philosophy at the University.

For some weeks the country remained more peaceful, but the shooting, by an opposition group, of a woman while a patient in hospital shocked many people. All the political talks and

148

conferences were not bringing any easing of the country's unrest. By December a rash of fire-bombs had devastated shopping areas in the city of Derry. Then a short ceasefire came for Christmas.

Early the following summer, Ray's two sisters, now on the Missions in India, came home again on holiday. They were pleased to find their mother in such good health after her bout of bronchitis earlier in the year. They were also excited about the imminent arrival of Father Stephen from South America. They looked well themselves and happy to see everyone, especially the children who had grown so much since their last visit. Kathleen's greeting of Leah was more casual these days, making her feel almost an accepted sister-in-law. But Eileen, brown eyes shining, showed as always her wonderful warmth of friendship.

They stayed at the bungalow and Leah, Ray and the children joined them there when they were not away visiting round the country. Some of their accounts of the hunger and disease among vast numbers of the Indian people, as well as the conflicts that arose between different sects, were most distressing. Another beautiful country, Leah thought, where so many people were living and dying in tragic circumstances - albeit of a different nature from the Troubles of her own land. And despite the many efforts being made in both these countries to stop the death and suffering, there seemed to be no real solution.

Father Stephen arrived to another great welcome. He looked a little older this time, his skin more weathered, his hair thinner and touched with white at the temples. He stayed at the farmhouse and the visiting and receiving of visitors continued. Each night the rosary was said for all those in trouble and for peace throughout the world.

There was further excitement when the three special guests attended church in their robes of office. Leah noted the pride and delight of Ray's mother and all the relations on seeing Father Stephen taking part in the services. Many of the churches were now supporting the Peace People, further prayers were being said everywhere, and, for a time, the news remained happier.

On suitable days, Father Stephen enjoyed giving a hand on the farm. He also drove around the country to see old friends. During a few quiet moments at home, Leah noticed her son Stephen's great pleasure as he showed his uncle his books, ready for another year's study. Once or twice, they talked well into the night and Father Stephen seemed most impressed by his nephew's progress at the University.

Soon the visitors had gone and the young people were back to their studies and sometimes helping with the harvest. In no time at all, Leah and Louise were making preparations for Christmas. As usual, Christmas Day was held for them all at the farmhouse.

Then, a few days before the celebrations began, several hotels were damaged by bombs and an announcement was made that there would be no cease-fire over the holiday period. This was a great disappointment and people remained nervous and unhappy into the New Year.

The next horrifying news came in mid-February when twelve people were killed and twenty-three injured in a restaurant destroyed by fire-bombs. This caused a widespread demand for an end to the campaign of violence. Talks started in great earnest among those in authority and Leah was hopeful that at last peace might come.

Patrick was now making an effort to prepare for his final school examination. He was nearly as tall as Stephen and more heavily built, with a healthy complexion from his outdoor activities. One evening as he sat studying, he suddenly announced to Leah and Ray that he would be glad to be giving up studying for good.

"I'm not much use at book work," he said. "And I don't know what I'm going to do when I leave school."

"Well, there's plenty of work to be done about here," Ray told him, looking rather surprised.

Patrick made no immediate response and Leah could see he was ill-at-ease. When he spoke, his face grew flushed. "You see," he said, slowly, "I've been wondering what Stephen's plans will be. Supposing he decides to come back home later on - to stay and work the farm and - well, maybe get married? What would happen to me then? I'm the one who should have a career." He sighed and, leaning his head on his hand, added disconsolately: "But working on the land is all I ever wanted to do."

Leah glanced thoughtfully at her worried-looking son, his eyes downcast.

Ray said, firmly: "Just concentrate on getting your exams, Patrick. Nobody knows for sure what the future may hold. But your mother and I are still in charge here and we hope to be for some time yet. In the meantime, we are counting on having your help. As you know, Davy will be leaving us next year to go to Australia. And if, as you say, Stephen should decide to come back here sometime later, we'll see that you still have plenty to do. You could, for instance, on a few acres, build up a thriving market garden - grow mushrooms - all sorts of things!"

Ray was smiling now. "Anyway, Patrick, don't you think something like that could solve your problem? Surely you know we would make sure you'd be all right."

Patrick nodded quickly, then said he was sorry and muttered his thanks. To hide his embarrassment, he opened a book and began to write rapidly.

Leah felt it was most unlike Patrick to be concerned about his future prospects. And she was not surprised to learn later that his wise friend, Robert Coulter, had warned him that, being a younger son, he might ultimately have to leave the home place. And what was he going to do, then?

Robert himself had finished with school and was quite the up-and-coming young farmer, dealing in his own cattle and sheep as well as helping his father. Leah remembered how he had started as a very young boy with a week-old calf which he had fed with milk in a bucket, at first letting the calf suck his immersed fingers, until it could manage to drink by itself.

Then each year when there were more than two lambs born to any of his father's sheep, he had reared the extra ones by feeding them similarly, or from a bottle - with ready help from his sisters. Tom and Muriel had found it happier for everyone to let Robert have his own livestock. He had an independent drive just like his grandmother Coulter. But as well, Leah knew, he had something of the kindly Linton nature.

Old Mrs Coulter had died the previous winter from pneumonia, after only a short illness. She had insisted on doing outside work in bitterly cold weather when it was evident it might be too much for her. Muriel and Tom had then moved into the main part of the house to care for Tom's father.

These evenings, Leah noticed that while Robert was calling ostensibly to see Patrick, it was Ruth who was getting most of his attention.

At nearly sixteen, she looked quite the young lady, with a mass of fair curls and vivid blue eyes that could show both her keen sense of humour and definite strength of mind.

Usually she was at the kitchen table doing her homework and Robert, instead of going off at once to find Patrick, was quite happy to sit watching her and to receive the occasional smile and word of recognition. He was delighted when she asked for his opinion on some mathematical problem and he was able to help.

During the following months, Robert often appeared in a smart sports jacket and clean shirt, his hair oiled and well-brushed. Muriel reported that he was putting his trousers under the mattress to keep them well-pressed. Patrick, still in jeans and working clothes had at first looked surprised and then annoyed.

"Where do you think you're going - all dressed up like that? And twice this week!"

Robert had muttered something about being in town earlier on business.

Leah had caught Ruth's eye and noted her amusement. Just lately, Muriel had spoken to Leah about this youthful romance and shown great interest.

"I used to hope so much that you and I would be related," Muriel reminded Leah, giving her a cautious, sideways glance. And now I'd be very happy if this should happen through our children." Then her smile suddenly faded. "But do you think that Ray approves of this friendship?"

"I don't think he takes it seriously," Leah said. "And neither does Ruth - I'm almost sure. She's still quite a child - more interested in getting her 'O' levels. When I mentioned Robert's obvious devotion, she merely looked amused and said: "Poor old Robert - he's really very nice. Did you know he's saving up to buy a second-hand car? He keeps asking if I'd come with him to a Y.F.C. hop somewhere out in the country."

Leah was reminded of the happy social evenings where she and Ray had first met. These gatherings of young farmers were no longer being held in the village hall. Attendance had gradually fallen off. The former trusting friendship between the two communities had suffered with the coming of the Troubles. And now Leah thought as Ray did that their young daughter should not go travelling about at night, even with Robert.

152

SEVENTEEN

There was great rejoicing later in the year when Patrick received his final examination results and found he had passed quite well.

"It was worth all that studying you put in," Ruth told him. "Now you can hold up your head with Robert."

But Patrick had his greatest wish of all; he was busy on the land, seeing to the harvest and the cattle, quite happy for the present to go on helping his father and to receive the pocket-money his parents could afford to give him. Urged on by Robert, he had bought two young calves to rear, and Ray had encouraged him to expand on this and any other ideas he might have.

Stephen, also, helped on the farm, mostly during holidays. Leah often looked out with something like wonder at the three men working happily together, and with whom she had so much in common. And she felt a gladness in her heart that life, despite many people's predictions, had so far treated them all so kindly.

Stephen still paid great attention to his studies and was now coaching some younger students. Helen had found him a room not far from the McCarroll home where he was always welcome. Like Robert, he now had a small car for coming home at weekends and for the occasional evening.

Sometimes he brought John McCarroll, Helen's older son, also at the University, and hoping to take a degree in Civil Engineering. His younger brother and sister were still at school. John seemed to enjoy a few hours helping in the fields and then joining the family for their evening meal. There was always much lively chatter and arguments, especially when Robert arrived, sometimes with his sisters, or Con looked in with his boys.

"You're very lucky around here," John remarked. "Everywhere is so quiet with no shooting or bombing to disturb or frighten you."

"Well," Ray said, frowning, "there have been one or two incidents - smashed windows in the village and a booby-trapped car that was luckily discovered in time."

"How would you like to hear explosions going off at close quarters, especially at night, as we have in the city?" Stephen put in.

Leah remembered these words some time later, shortly after the New Year celebrations. She was at the top of the stairs, about to go to bed, when she stood stock still, shocked and terrified by a thunderous bang that seemed to shake the very foundations of the house. Her heart plunged painfully, leaving her weak and trembling.

Then with Ray and the children she hurried to a front bedroom window to gaze out in wide-eyed horror at the massive flames and brilliant glow rising high into the star-lit darkness some distance beyond the Lintons' house. She had heard of explosions and death in other places, she had seen the devastation on television. But this was here and now - happening before her very eyes.

"It sounded just beside us!" Ruth whispered, her eyes stricken.

"They've bombed a building in the village," Ray said, moving away quickly. "I must get in touch with Jim; we'll try to help."

Patrick looked worried. "But Dad - will people think we had something to do with this?"

Ray turned at the door, his eyes stern. "Patrick - I think everyone about here knows we are Nationalists; they also know we would never do anything like this."

When Ray had gone, Leah stood with the children watching ambulances, fire-brigades and cars racing past. No-one in or around the village would be sleeping that night. Gradually they saw the brilliance in the sky fading into showers of sparks and swirling clouds of smoke. Leah tried to shut out horrifying images of dead and injured bodies as she made some tea and wondered what was happening to their shattered village.

When the phone rang they all looked startled. It was Muriel to say that three people had been taken to hospital, but it was hoped their lives were not in danger. Those with minor injuries, like cuts and bruises had been seen by a doctor and nurse. One building had been almost demolished and two adjacent houses had roof and window damage. Ray and other helpers were still clearing up. "We never thought that anything like this would happen here," Muriel said.

Ray arrived much later, his face grim and streaked with soot. He said that those affected by the explosion had been settled in somewhere for the night, and further work on damaged houses would continue in the morning. He said it was a miracle that people had not been killed. As it was, he wasn't likely to forget the shocked and bewildered eyes of the very elderly couple, or the terrified cries of some little children, all of whom had been taken from their beds in the midst of the holocaust.

This savage attack on the village was the main topic of conversation for a very long time, and the people living there remained anxiously suspicious of any unusual movements or strangers about the place as the rebuilding went on.

Further bombing and killing continued in other places. But the news that Pope John Paul II was coming on a pastoral visit to Ireland had given great hope and pleasure throughout much of the country.

Several of Ray's relations spoke to Leah of what this event meant to them, and they were among the thousands who travelled to Dublin to see and hear the head of their Church at the huge gathering in Phoenix Park.

Leah and the family watched all the proceedings on television. People were greatly moved by the events of the visit and felt that a real opportunity had been created to end the violence which the Pope had so strongly condemned. However, certain elements throughout the land were set on another course and so the Troubles continued.

Soon Stephen was in his final year at the University, and Ruth had begun her teacher-training course at the College at Stranmillis. Stephen brought her home sometimes and, when she was to play in a week-end tennis match, Robert came for her. Her shorter free-times were divided between Helen's family and her grandparents. When Leah questioned her about this latter arrangement, she merely looked amused.

"Oh, Grandad would probably have a fit if he knew where I go after visiting him. But what he doesn't know won't do him any harm! Anyway, to me Helen's home is not unlike my own. But Grandad acts as though I have no home."

Leah knew that her father deliberately ignored the existence of Ruth's family. As far as he was concerned, he had no daughter or any other grandchildren.

Since the coming of the Troubles, the city had changed greatly from the quiet days of Leah's own childhood, and she and Ray were relieved to know that Ruth had so many friends. She was also anxious about her parents; her father was now ninety, her mother eighty. But at last they were accepting daily help in the house and Aunt Emily saw them quite often.

At Easter, Aunt Emily's daughter, Carol, and grand-daughter, Claire, were over from England. Ruth and Claire, both training to become teachers, soon found they had much in common, and Ruth promised to spend a week or so at Claire's home in the summer.

Like Stephen, Ruth never neglected her studies and Leah was soon looking forward to the possibility of her daughter teaching in a school near her home. She also hoped that in time Ruth and Robert might be married. He was still most attentive when Ruth was around. Patrick had long ago widened his circle of friends and often borrowed the car to go off to see neighbouring young farmers or to spend an evening in the town. And Ruth spent much of her time at the Coulter house during holidays. Anne and Joan were usually there and they all played tennis or Robert took them out for the evening.

Muriel reported that Ruth was a great tease. "I'm sure Robert wonders sometimes how she really regards him. I just wish she would give him a little encouragement now and again. When that friend of Stephen's brought her home from the city a few times, Robert seemed upset. 'You could have 'phoned that you were getting home early,' he told her, 'and I would have come for you.' But Ruth gave him her usual dismissive answer: 'Just remember, Robert Coulter, that you don't own me!' And, of course, she says it all with apparent good humour."

Leah and Muriel decided that Ruth's flippancy was probably an attempt to hide her real feelings, to delay having to make any important decisions when her mind, for the present, was on other matters. And Leah thought it better not to question her.

One evening, Stephen rang to say he was coming home for an hour or so as he had something important to tell his parents.

"It's something I have wanted to tell you both for quite a long time."

When Stephen arrived, he stood in the hallway regarding Leah anxiously, a little sadly.

"It can't be as bad as all that!" she said, brightly. "Perhaps it would be easier for you to have a talk with your father first?"

When the two men went off together, Leah recalled that for some time Stephen seemed to have had something on his mind over and above his studies. During the previous holidays he had appeared unusually preoccupied and withdrawn from the family. He had watched eagerly for letters coming. Then one or two official-looking envelopes had arrived and his uncle had written from South America. These seemingly had helped to settle some problem that apparently he had felt was outside his parents experience.

Nearly an hour later, Stephen came to say goodbye, and Leah saw at once that much of the strain had left his eyes. "Dad will tell you everything," he told her. "He feels sure you will understand. I can only hope you will." There was an excitement in him now.

Leah smiled. "Don't worry, Stephen. I think I know already what this is all about." As for her own feelings in the matter, she wasn't quite sure.

She and Ray waved their son goodbye. They then sat together in the growing darkness watching from a window as his car disappeared.

"I suppose, like me," Ray said, "you may have thought that Stephen was worried about his final examinations. But it isn't that at all." He pressed her hand in a consoling gesture.

Leah said, with an air of resignation: "I believe you're going to tell me that our son wishes to become a priest."

"Leah - you knew!" Ray eyes had widened in surprise. "And Stephen's big worry was that you might be upset."

"I only guessed - I thought it was a possibility."

"And how do you feel about it - now that you know?"

"If Stephen has decided he has a true calling for this work, it's only right he should go ahead. It's in the family tradition and will meet with great approval, especially from your mother."

Ray nodded. "Yes, and Stephen thinks she knows something about his plans from Father Stephen."

Leah thought of old Mrs Anderson now in her eighties and confined to bed for the past few weeks, still very weak from her latest attack of bronchitis. She loved talking to Stephen about her own son's work and she, too, watched for his letters coming.

"Of course," Ray was saying, "Stephen will have to put in many years of training at a seminary. Even then, he may not be accepted as someone suitable for the priesthood."

As he spoke of the long training and the dedicated life that lay before their son, Leah's mind was trying to block out the cold and bitter gaze of her father as she had last seen him in his little church hall. She felt thankful that he need never know the life's work chosen by one of his grandsons.

For herself, religious practice had no set programme, no special name. Christianity, she believed, should be woven into everyday living; a constant prayer for good to prevail over evil, for equality among peoples and thankfulness for our amazing and wonderful world, which properly managed would provide for everyone. Sadly, this was not happening.

Leah felt sorrow, too, for her own divided family; divided, not merely by different forms of Christianity, with their worldly standards and opinions, but by prejudices and misunderstandings through centuries of complicated history.

EIGHTEEN

During Ruth's last year at the Training College she did not come home so often and Leah worried about her.

"I've work to do, haven't I?" she said when questioned. Then as though regretting the impatient note in her voice, she added: "Helen's very good to me; the whole family are; I can call with them any time. And Grandad hasn't been so well lately. So I take the bus to see him at weekends and sometimes after lectures."

Leah thought that Ruth and Robert probably 'phoned each other. And he might take her out sometimes. Ruth rarely spoke of her private life, yet Leah felt she was happy enough in her own quiet way. But she was greatly disappointed to hear from Muriel that she did not think Ruth and Robert were in touch very often.

"It's beginning to look as though Robert isn't going to wait around any longer for Ruth to make up her mind about him. Anne tells me that, for some time past, he has been leaving that young girl, Caroline Henry, home from the church choir-practice. And someone saw them together in the town the other night. You know Caroline, don't you? She's Sam and Mavis Henry's only child - a very nice wee girl. She and Joan were at school together. The Henry place is a couple of miles out our way; you couldn't miss it with their big herd of Friesian cows blocking the road at milking times."

"Anyway, Robert tells us nothing these days. We have no idea where he is many evenings."

This news worried Leah. The whole family liked Robert. It had pleased her when even her father had taken to him and thought him a proper friend for Ruth. Robert had told the old man about modern methods of farming that meant a much easier life than during his days on the land.

It was true that Ruth seemed to have treated Robert in a rather offhand manner, but that was how she dealt with Patrick and many of her friends, lately. And Robert had been around for so long they all thought of him as almost one of the family.

When Ruth did come home at holiday times, she brought books to study and spent most of the day shut away by herself. But Leah often heard her radio tuned-in to 'Country and Western' and all the popular romantic music. She went out a few evenings when Robert and Anne called for her.

With Patrick out in the evenings and Stephen away, Leah and Ray had seen little of Robert, themselves. They were beginning to feel a new freedom about their own lives which they found quite pleasant. They were able to see friends more often and do things they previously had little time for, like Leah's love of growing begonias, indoor and out, and their other plans for the house and garden, including the building of a sizeable greenhouse.

Louise and Dermot were to be married soon and, while someone sat with old Mrs Anderson, Leah and Louise went shopping. As Ray's mother was often in bed these days, it was to be a quiet wedding and Louise and Dermot would live at the bungalow during the old lady's life-time. Later on, they would move to a new house that Dermot was planning to build on his farm.

One evening, Leah and Ray had an unexpected visitor. John McCarroll, whom they had not seen so often since Stephen had left for the seminary, arrived driving his father's car. Leah and Ray with Helen and Sean had attended the graduation ceremony of the two friends. Since then John had had only a few temporary jobs: in the Post Office at Christmas and doing holiday work at one or two petrol stations. Helen had told them he was still applying for any positions that seemed suitable, but there were very few vacancies for civil engineers.

On seeing Leah and Ray in the front garden, John raised a hand and smiled. As he walked towards them, Leah noticed how Helen's elder son had grown up in the past year. He had his mother's straight carriage and dark colouring, his father's attractive smile, and now there was an added assurance about him.

"I've come to say goodbye," he said. "I've found some work at last." He paused a moment and then added - "in England, in Birmingham, with a large engineering firm. My parents are very pleased and I've written to Stephen; he advised me to apply for work in England."

"It's certainly great news," Ray said, and he and Leah wished him well for the future. "This calls for a celebration; we'll get Patrick to join us." And they moved towards the house.

"Everyone says I'm lucky to be getting away from the Troubles here," John told them. "But it's going to be quite a wrench leaving all my friends." Leah heard his sudden sigh. "Of course," he went on, "it will be great to have a job - and I'll be home whenever possible." His eyes lit up again.

John stayed for their evening meal. Then he and Patrick went off for a run into the country. Leah watched them go. "John seemed strangely uneasy," she remarked. "Helen always said he was a real home bird. Perhaps that's the trouble?"

With the start of summer weather, Ray and Patrick were soon busy in the fields with hay and silage making. Leah had her poultry and the garden to see to during spare moments from the house. She wondered often how Ruth was getting on. They heard from her now and again, but had not seen her for some time as she was now studying hard. Then, one afternoon, she rang to say her exams were all over. But before coming home, she intended to spend a day or so with her grandparents. She would leave her luggage at Helen's and hope that Patrick could come to collect her.

Leah was excited and yet a little anxious at the thought of having Ruth about the house again. They had grown apart with the long separation, and now she and Ray were out of touch with their daughter's life and interests. Perhaps things would improve now they were to be together again. Leah, although she had not been asked to do so, had been looking in local papers for teaching vacancies suitable for Ruth - and within reasonable distance of her home. So far nothing suitable had appeared.

When Ruth suddenly arrived, Leah was delighted to see it was Robert who had brought her.

"Wasn't I lucky," Ruth called to her, "Robert was going to the city today and Anne rang to tell me. So here I am."

The car was packed with cases, books and an assortment of property. Leah watched as the two young ones, laughing and joking, carried things into the house. Then Ray and Patrick joined them for afternoon tea, and soon Robert left. Ruth thanked him for all his help and said she hoped to call when Anne was home from her hospital work in two days' time.

"What I want now is a lovely, long rest," Ruth said.

"We'll come for you," Robert told her, "as soon as Anne arrives."

Leah smiled. Everything was working out just as she had hoped.

During the following weeks Leah was pleased to see Ruth so often in the garden. She no longer looked so pale and tired from studying.

She spent hours weeding and helping to pick the blackcurrants and the raspberries that were sold to Muriel's cousin for their shop in town.

Leah sometimes wondered why Ruth was not making a greater effort to find a teaching post. She said, when asked, that nothing really suitable had come to her notice. She wrote lots of letters, but they seemed to be mostly to friends she had made. Every week or so she went to see her grandparents and to call with Helen's family and girls she now knew in the city.

And Ruth still joined the Coulters and others on the tennis courts. She went out for evenings in the town, and Robert or Anne, or both of them, left her home. Leah longed to ask if Caroline Henry had been one of their party. Ruth had already mentioned that Caroline played tennis with them and sometimes was at the Coulter house along with others when she herself arrived.

On Leah's next meeting with Muriel, she could not resist asking if there was any further news of Caroline and Robert.

"I've no idea what's going on," Muriel told her. "They all seem very happy together - dashing off here and there. Only time will tell."

Ruth usually accompanied Leah and Ray on family visits into the country or down to see the Lintons. Lindy's and Jim's two young daughters were already very fashion-conscious and most interested in disco-dancing. They amused Ruth greatly as they plied her with questions about all that was happening in the city regarding these matters.

Ruth also liked to visit her Grandmother Anderson. And after Louise and Dermot were married she often kept her company when they were out together.

One afternoon Leah found Ruth sitting on the garden seat staring

162

into space. She had spent a busy morning picking gooseberries.

Leah was carrying the local newspaper that Patrick had just brought home. "You'll be interested in this," she said, in some excitement, pointing to the column headed 'Education'. "Look - a teaching vacancy only three or four miles away."

Ruth read through the paragraph but showed little reaction.

"You may not think so, Mother," she said slowly, looking up, "but I have been giving a lot of thought to the future. And I'm not so sure it's a good idea for me to be applying for a teaching post in this area."

Leah regarded her daughter in some puzzlement. "You mean - you would rather not be near your own home?" Leah could see all her hopes and plans fading.

"It's not that exactly," Ruth answered. "I've been wondering - perhaps I might not be accepted around here. Not every Protestant teacher has a priest and nuns among her relations."

"Oh, Ruth - you can't mean that people would object to your father's family?"

Ruth shrugged. "There are some people, I fear, who would question my suitability - my loyalty, even - with the background that I have."

"I'm sure you're wrong about that," Leah said quickly. She suddenly had a wonderful idea: if Ruth were married to Robert it might make a difference. She was about to suggest this to Ruth when something stopped her. Ruth had become even more reticent lately about her affairs. It would not do to rush her. Clearly, she needed time before committing herself to any action involving her future.

Ruth folded the paper. "I think I'd be better off somewhere else, Mother, perhaps in the anonymity of a town or a city where no one bothers so much about one's family background."

"Well, there's no hurry, dear, to do anything." Leah smiled her encouragement. "You know we are very happy to have you at home as long as you're content to stay. But I think you are wrong to dismiss any chance you may have of employment about here."

When Leah told Ray of Ruth's reluctance to apply for a position in a local school, he agreed she was being far too sensitive about her family connections.

"It's not like Ruth at all," he said. "Anyway, it's best to leave her

163

to her own devices for the present. But I hope she realises it's not easy these days to get work just where and when you want it."

"Well, I can't help thinking," Leah said, "that Ruth has something else on her mind. There's something that seems to be worrying her."

Following this, with no one pressing her to find employment, Ruth was in a much happier mood. She played tapes of pop music from Patrick's collection. Then she started on Leah's and Ray's records and the house was filled with music. Sometimes they heard the lilting waltzes of Strauss, Chopin and Lehar, or it might be some of the songs from the great musical shows they had seen on family outings. They included: 'Oh, What A Beautiful Mornin'', 'Waltz Of My Heart', 'We'll Gather Lilacs', and 'I Whistle A Happy Tune'. These she played over and over again.

There was also the radio where Ruth listened to programmes of old-time music. Leah would hear Jim Reeves singing: 'Have You Ever Been Lonely?' or Andy Williams with: 'Can't Help Falling In Love With You'.

Some of these tunes from the past, like 'Tulips From Amsterdam' and 'Around The World I've Searched For You', sent Leah herself waltzing round the kitchen, her heart and eyes full of memories. She could only hope that some day Ruth would find the happiness that she and Ray had enjoyed despite the many barriers trying to divide them. She wished so much that something would be settled soon between Ruth and Robert.

Ruth was still seeing Robert quite often, but neither Leah nor Muriel knew whether or not their friendship was making any real progress.

When Robert went to the city on a business trip, Ruth went with him. And when he called for her later at her grandparents' house, he always stayed for a chat. Leah knew, from her mother's guarded remarks that both her parents would be very happy to accept Robert as a husband for Ruth.

After her last visit to the city, Ruth had reported that her grandfather was not so well. She had found him in bed and looking very tired and frail. "He fell asleep while I was reading to him from Psalm twenty-five, one of his favourites. Poor Granny is worried about him."

A few days later Aunt Emily 'phoned to tell Leah her father was a little better and was up again. She had called to see Leah's parents on her way home from England after visiting her daughter in Stafford. Her grand-daughter, Claire, had just returned from a holiday in France and would be in touch soon with Ruth.

Leah suggested to Ruth that she too might like to go on holiday - perhaps with Anne or some other friend. They themselves would not be able to get away until the harvest was safely in. Leah also knew that young people liked to get away on their own. But Ruth assured her parents that she did not need a holiday.

Two days later, when she received an invitation from Claire to join her for a week or so in England, Ruth quickly changed her mind.

Soon she was rushing around getting ready, singing and dancing through the house. Leah was very pleased to see Ruth so enthusiastic about something again, even though it was only a holiday.

Leah and Ray took Ruth to the cross-channel boat. Driving along, they heard her humming happy tunes like: 'Thank you for the music' and 'I'd like to teach the world to sing'. She drew their attention to lovely views of mountain and river, to splendid fields of golden crops waiting to be harvested.

Approaching built-up areas, rose-filled gardens caught her eye, and then the play of sunlight and shadow across the hills high above the city. Today, Ruth saw only the beautiful things.

Later, as they waved her goodbye, Leah smiled at Ray as she remarked: "I think Ruth is really happy to be getting away from us all!"

It had been some time since Leah and Ray had visited the city and now they looked about them in surprise at all the changes that had taken place. Whole rows of remembered streets and some factories had vanished as a result of bombing or re-development, or both, leaving great open spaces and often exposing other unsightly buildings. Slogans and graffiti abounded, of a nature calculated to give offence and provoke one side of the community or the other.

But there were also some pleasant surprises. New and imposing office buildings had been erected. There were many new dwelling houses, looking neat and attractive with gardens already producing flowers and shrubs.

As they had promised, Leah and Ray drove to see Helen and Sean. Their daughter was on holiday in County Clare and their student son, Aidan, was working in a local hotel. "And we're looking forward to having John home from England very soon," Helen said. "Thank goodness he seems to be settling down at last to his new life over there. He doesn't write often but he says he has lots to tell us."

"And we hope to have Stephen home, shortly, for a visit," Leah said. "He'll be delighted to see John again. You must all take a day to the country for a grand reunion - though I'm not sure when Ruth intends to return."

Back at the farm, Leah and Ray found the house very empty and quiet without Ruth, especially the bright, lively girl she had recently become. Later that night she telephoned to say she had arrived safely and would be leaving at the weekend to go to the family cottage at the coast with Claire and two friends. They were not to worry about her.

Leah smiled, hearing the note of happiness and excitement in her daughter's voice. At last Ruth was getting the holiday she needed and deserved. From the excellent results she had obtained in her Final examinations Leah knew that Ruth must have studied very hard over her last few months. She needed this holiday and, when she came home again, well-rested, she would see her future in a different light.

NINETEEN

One evening, a week or so later, Aunt Emily arrived in her little blue Mini. She had been to see Leah's parents that afternoon. As she came in, Leah saw that her face lacked the usual smile.

"I'm afraid your father has taken a turn for the worse, Leah. Your mother is very worried about him. He keeps asking for Ruth and we are unable to get in touch with her. It seems all the family in England are away on holiday. Your mother will 'phone you after the doctor's visit tomorrow."

Aunt Emily looked tired. Leah made some tea for her before she set off again to stay with her daughter, Jane, for a day or two, as promised.

"I'm feeling my age," Aunt Emily said. "I'm thinking of giving up the car at the end of the year. I've had one or two frights lately. The present day traffic moves much too fast for me!"

As Leah waved her goodbye and wished her a safe journey, she suddenly realised that her aunt was now eighty years of age. Yet she was still very active. Leah also remembered how her wonderfully kind aunt had helped her through so many difficulties over the years. She had been a great friend to both Ray and herself. What would she have done without her?

Early the following morning, Leah's mother telephoned to say her father was gravely ill. "The doctor has told me he could last several weeks or maybe only a few days. All he asks for is to see Ruth. I wish she would come. We have had a card from her, saying: 'See you soon.' But no definite date was given for her return."

"I think she intended to come home this weekend," was all Leah could tell her. She, too, had received only a brief message. Yet, the previous year, Ruth had sent cards home with tightly written news of all her adventures with Claire and her friends.

"I've been wondering," Leah's mother went on, and now her voice held a cautious note, "if you could come here yourself, Leah? In his present state, your poor father has no idea who is in the house. So you need have no fear about upsetting him. I'd like to have you while Emily is away - in case anything should happen."

That afternoon, Ray drove Leah to her parents' home and went in for the very first time. Leah's mother, looking pale and worried greeted them hurriedly, explaining that she was about to join a visitor from their church in the sick-room. She thanked Ray for coming so promptly and made him come in. Then she left, saying she would see them shortly.

Leah's heart was thumping nervously as they passed her father's door. She gazed around her old home and looked into rooms, surprised to see how few changes had been made during all the years she had been away. Ruth, of course, who knew the place so well, had kept the old home fresh in her mind.

And now, quickly, with a feeling of guilt, as though someone might be about to stop her, Leah began pointing out to Ray some of the specially remembered things from her youth; pictures, ornaments, her mother's harmonium and sewing machine, her father's large Bible, as always, on the table near the window among piles of coloured religious tracts, writings and notes.

Through the kitchen window, she stared at the garden where neat bushes and hedges of the past had grown tall and unrestrained. But the greenhouse, now partly hidden, seemed much smaller and in need of paint. Everywhere she looked was taking her back so many years, stirring up the past, making her heart and pulses race and throb in some confusion, so that nothing seemed quite real.

Had she done something so terribly wrong in leaving her home, ignoring her parents' teaching and their inflexible wishes regarding her future? She had no answer to that. She had done only what her heart had told her.

Ray touched her arm. "Are you all right, Leah? You were shaking your head, dear." His eyes were full of concern.

"I was - just thinking - about everything." She knew that Ray would understand. His life, too, had been influenced and conditioned by so much of her past and the events that had happened during their years together.

He nodded. And now she saw how uneasy he looked.

"I feel I should go," he said, moving into the hallway. "It isn't right for me to be here, Leah, when I know your father's wishes."

And I'm not wanted, either, Leah thought sadly, as she followed Ray to say goodbye. "I'll 'phone you later on," she whispered, reluctant to let him go. As the car moved off, she waved, and a strange loneliness gripped her. She closed the door quietly and then stood listening.

From her father's room she could hear low voices. And as she passed the slightly open door, she could see a stout, grey-haired man in a dark suit rising from where he had been kneeling at the bedside.

"I think he's asleep again," the man said quietly to Leah's mother as he lifted his Bible and prepared to leave.

Leah slipped into the little back bedroom that had once been hers. How strange it was to see some of Ruth's things among those of her own, one-time possessions, left behind so suddenly and finally on that fateful day so long ago.

She recognised her daughter's silver bangle, a pink comb, a tiny bottle of scent, all laid out on the linen runner she herself had helped her mother to embroider with rows of sunflowers and green leaves. And there on the tallboy sat her old teddy bear, newly clad in a red jersey and grey shorts. She had loved that teddy during her early years when life had seemed to hold no problems and she and her parents had been happy together. But Ruth had come to them - to love the teddy, too, and bring some happiness into their home. Leah felt grateful that this had been possible.

As she gazed around, memories came flooding back bringing further pangs of sadness. Her old school books still sat on the shelf above the little table where she had often studied. But the typewriter had gone - donated by her father long ago for use at the church.

She was standing holding a tiny blue and white cup-and-saucer from her childhood tea-set when her mother appeared at the door.

"Poor Leah," she said. "It has been such a long time, hasn't it ?"

Her mother looked strained and ill as she told her that her father had now fallen into a deep sleep. "You could come along and see him quite safely, dear. I think you should."

For a moment, Leah held her breath, considering what to do.

"Well - not yet," she said. "Perhaps later on. I don't feel quite ready." She was remembering her father's cruel coldness on their last meeting years ago. It would always be fresh in her mind.

"I think you should have a rest," Leah told her mother. "I'm here now to answer the door and the 'phone and do anything I can."

Her mother looked grateful. "Perhaps I will lie down for a while. But you must call me right away if you think your father is awake."

Some minutes later, Leah stood outside her father's room, ears strained for any sound. Heart thumping, she gently pushed open the door a further few inches. The head of the bed was towards her, just as she remembered it. She could hear her father's rather laboured breathing and, after a few anxious seconds, she tip-toed nearer, eyes and ears strained to catch the slightest change in his condition.

Leah scarcely recognised the pale, lined face on the pillow. Her father's eyes were deeply sunken, his cheeks hollow. She could understand her mother's great concern about him. As though sensing someone's presence, he suddenly stirred and moaned a little.

For a moment, Leah froze in fright. Then, as she quickly crouched beside the bed, one thin, bony hand slid over the edge towards her making her heart plunge painfully. She waited nervously until her father's faint, intermittent breathing was resumed and, drawing on all her courage, she gently lifted his limp fingers and replaced them on the covers.

As she tried to withdraw her hand, a slight pressure held her there, and she waited, overcome with an emotion compounded of panic and pity.

Suddenly, her father's eyes were wide open. For a moment, he stared straight at her. Then the eye-lids closed again on the lightest of sighs. Leah was still in a state of shock, watching him, when she saw his pale lips moving and heard his faltering voice:

"My - own - girl. So glad - you've come."

Leah's heart seemed to swell with a wild happiness, so overpowering she could scarcely see through her tears as she waited, hoping he would speak to her again. Then his fingers, resting in hers, relaxed their hold and soon his breathing told her he had slipped back into sleep.

170

But her father had spoken the words she had been longing to hear and she was filled with a sense of elation. She had been forgiven, accepted at last! This would be wonderful news for her mother, too.

Her father's aged face on the pillow looked more peaceful now with a new serenity. Leah, deeply moved, her face flushed, quietly left the room.

At the door, the ringing of the 'phone startled her. It also alerted her mother who came hurrying from the spare room to take the call.

Leah waiting anxiously, soon gathered that it was good news from England, and her excitement increased.

"Yes," her mother said, replacing the receiver and looking greatly relieved, "that was to say the girls were on their way home and Ruth should arrive here early tomorrow."

Leah could scarcely wait to tell her own story. "Oh, Mother," she began, "something wonderful has -" But her mother was already hurrying away to listen at her father's door.

"Still sleeping, I think," she said in a low voice. "But I'd better make sure." And she vanished inside.

Leah stood waiting, even more impatiently excited, wondering what was happening and if her father might ask for her again.

Several minutes passed before her mother's return. "I'm so glad I went in," she said. "Your poor father woke up for a few seconds and, at first, I thought his mind was wandering. But, of course, he had only been dreaming." She gave Leah a sad little smile. "Poor Matthew - he thought that Ruth had been in to see him! He struggled to tell me and was so pleased when I said he would see her again very soon, God willing. I gave him a sip of water and he closed his eyes. He'll sleep more peacefully now, I'm sure." She paused, looking at Leah thoughtfully. "This would be a good time for you to see your father, Leah."

"No - no! I can't," Leah said, turning aside quickly. Her face had gone cold at her mother's disclosure and a heaviness dragged at her heart. How foolish she had been.

Leah felt now that her father in his weak state must have mistaken her for Ruth, that was all. There had been no forgiveness, no acceptance; there never would be any now.

"I'll make a cup of tea," she called, hurrying into the kitchen, her eyes filling with tears.

171

When the doctor returned that evening, he told Leah's mother there appeared to be a slight improvement in the patient. "He's brighter, more alert, I think. You should get some rest yourself. Nurse will see to everything for the night. And she'll call you if necessary."

Leah was glad to hear that her aunt was expected the following day. She rang Ray and told him the latest news and of their hope that Ruth would arrive in the morning. She would tell him sometime later about seeing her father and of her great disappointment.

It was after midnight before Leah could persuade her mother to leave the kindly nurse in charge and retire to bed, at least for an hour or two. She herself lay awake for a long time going over and over those few moments with her father when she had felt absolutely sure he had recognised her. Perhaps he had? Would he have spoken to Ruth using those very same words?

It was a knocking on her door towards daylight that told her she had finally fallen asleep. Suddenly she was fully alert, sensing that something had happened.

"I'm sorry to have to tell you," the nurse said quietly, "that your father passed away peacefully in his sleep a short time ago."

Leah's thoughts were now for her mother. But she found her quite calm.

"It was all over very quickly," she said. "There was no time to call you. He died happy, I know, still believing he had seen Ruth. He loved her dearly. They were always such good friends."

Leah felt saddened as she listened. She could not help thinking of all the distress and even cruelty being caused throughout the country because friendship and understanding between certain people of the two communities were being withheld in the name of religious and political differences. Surely such a way of life was against all Christian values? And this was how her own father had chosen to live - cut off from his own family. Yet, in her heart, Leah knew she could no longer regret that last encounter with her dying father. How could she - when it had brought such happiness to his final hours?

Aunt Emily was the first to arrive that morning and soon she was helping with all the arrangements that had to be made, the 'phoning to be done.

A short time later, Leah heard her calling in some excitement from the front room: "Ruth has arrived! Here she is - looking all bright-eyed and sunburnt. Oh, poor Ruth, she'll be so disappointed to hear she didn't make it in time. She must have got a lift from the boat. A young man brought her. He left her case on the step and then drove off."

Leah's mother was already at the door speaking quietly to Ruth as she brought her in, breaking gently what had happened during the night.

"Oh, poor, poor Grandad," Ruth kept saying, suddenly in tears when she learned how happy he had been believing he had seen his grand-daughter before he died.

Leah now went forward to greet Ruth who stared at her in surprise.

"Mother - you're here! I didn't expect -"

Leah said sadly: "Your Grandfather was already too ill to really know who was in the house. And mother was on her own."

"I do wish I'd come sooner," Ruth said, regretfully. "I can scarcely believe that Grandfather has gone. He was always so good and kind to me."

She paused for a moment. Then she looked at Leah, sighed and said: "But he was very cruel to the rest of my family; he refused to have any friendship with those of the Catholic faith. And he was so very much mistaken about people like Daddy. I could only feel sorry for him - he missed so much in life."

"And he almost reached the age of ninety-five," Aunt Emily reminded them. "Not many live as long as that."

And Leah found herself thinking how easy it would have been for such an old man, his sight now dim, his mind fading, to have mistaken her for Ruth. She would have to accept that this was what had happened.

All her father's life had been governed by fixed ideas and rules and about these he had always remained unshakable. Was he likely to have changed towards her in the last moments of his life? That was something she would never know.

TWENTY

Leah attended her father's funeral with her mother and Ruth, Aunt Emily and a few relations and friends. He was buried beside his parents in the country graveyard of the old church near the family home.

It seemed to Leah only right that she should be present in spite of all that had happened. As she read the names on some of the older tombstones among ancient cypresses, laurel bushes and newly mown grass, she realised this was the final resting place of many of her ancestors. And this was her own father who was being laid to rest today.

Ray had not come with them. Leah's mother and Aunt Emily had agreed that it would not be quite seemly - considering everything.

When the grave-side service was over and the other mourners had left on the forty-mile journey back to the city, Leah and Ruth made a few inquiries from the elderly sexton about her father's old home and the people who now owned it.

The man's eyes lit up with interest as he told them that the farm still belonged to the Hamilton family who had bought it from her father and his brother years ago. "They've looked after it well and, just lately, built on a big kitchen with all them modern gadgets." He pointed across some fields. "There - you can see it, that long low house with cream walls and red roof. It's not far from the Garveys' place further up the hill."

A look of curiosity came over the sexton's face as he regarded Leah. "Did you know the Garveys were relations of yours? Your father's sister, dead these few years, was married to old Sean Garvey. He's gone too. There was no love lost between their two families, I can tell you." Before he could continue on the subject of the 'mixed marriage', Leah thanked him for his kindness and she and Ruth left.

She remembered very well Aunt Emily's story years ago of how her father and his brother, when selling the home place, had made sure the Garveys did not get the land to add to their own adjoining farm. But today was not the time to be talking of such things. Later on, it might be pleasant to come back with Ray and the family, perhaps to call at both houses and make themselves known - in a spirit of friendliness.

Driving home, Leah realised that Ruth was sunk in thought beside her and showing some reluctance to talk about the day's happenings. She herself was soon reviewing all that had taken place, from the service at the grave-side when two or three local people had come to join them.

Leah knew her tears had come mainly for what she considered to be her father's wasted years. He had used, so mistakenly, the greatest influence in his life, his religion, to bring pain and sorrow to himself and others - instead of showing a true spirit of fellowship and real understanding.

There was too much pain and sorrow around these days, Leah thought sadly, and helping to add to it would never resolve any of the country's Troubles. People like her father, on either side of the community, holding such strongly biased religious and political views, were partly responsible for the terrible things that had happened to their country and its people. And this state of affairs seemed likely to continue. Only a true friendship between the two communities could bring about real peace.

As they drew nearer home, Ruth suddenly became more talkative. Leah was surprised to hear her again on the subject of her grandfather's treatment of their family. After all, this was the day of his funeral and he had cared deeply for Ruth. Leah thought she might have postponed this talk until sometime later.

"Deep bitterness like Grandad's," Ruth continued, "goes far back into history. I knew he would never change. I also knew that you had sent me to him in an effort to ease the great tragedy of his life - your marriage to Daddy, whom he saw only as an enemy of the Protestant people."

Leah said quietly: "How wrong he was to regard your kind and honourable father as an enemy."

Ruth nodded her agreement. "Of course, in fairness," she said, frowning, "the strife and bitterness has not been one-sided.

175

Religious differences have kept our two communities apart for centuries."

Again, Leah felt that these pronouncements, coming from Ruth were most unusual, and especially today. She was probably more upset than they had thought. Or - at last she felt freer to speak her thoughts.

However, it was wonderful to have her home again and to see her looking so well. Even in her thoughtful moods there was a glow about her, fair curls shining and fashionably styled, eyes softly bright. Today she was wearing her smart navy dress with its wide, white collar and pleated skirt, bought recently for her cousin Adam's wedding. Ruth, getting ready that morning, had admired Leah's blue-grey summer suit and had adjusted her wide-brimmed navy straw hat "to a better angle and to show your hair!" Leah's hair had darkened over the years and lately she had noticed the occasional grey strand.

And now her daughter was again in thoughtful mood. Leah called out: "We'll soon be home. I'm sure they are wondering about us."

Ruth did not answer at once. When she spoke there was a note of caution in her voice. "Mother," she said, "I can only stay at home a day or two. You see, I have arranged now to return to England."

"But, Ruth - not for long I hope. You could be missing - well - some teaching post -" Her voice trailed away. "Anyway, we'd be very glad to have you at home; you know that." Leah felt strangely worried.

"I have been offered a job," Ruth said. "At least for some months - to teach a young boy who is convalescing after an operation. Something else could turn up after that."

"But is it wise, dear? I mean, to leave here and everyone you know?"

"I think so." Ruth answered. "You see there's something else I have to tell you - when we get home. Dad must hear this, too."

As they drove on, Ruth said nothing more. Leah felt mystified and rather uneasy. Soon they were through the village and, with relief, she saw Ray watching for them at the front of the house.

"Everything went very well," she told him. "My poor father is now at peace. I'll tell you all about it later."

"Your mother 'phoned," he said. "They all got home safely and she is going to stay with Aunt Emily for some time."

"I'm very glad," Leah said. "She really needs to get away. I'll just let her know we have arrived."

Leah then called Ray and Ruth to the sitting room and they all sat down looking rather solemn. She sighed and said: "Ruth has something important she wants to tell us. And I'm disappointed to hear she intends to return almost immediately to work in England."

"Oh, no, Ruth," her father said, frowning, "why this sudden notion?"

"Please, you two - don't look so upset," Ruth begged them, glancing into the garden from her seat near the window. "I'm truly sorry I have to bring this up today."

Ruth turned and regarded them a little sadly. "I have wanted to tell you the whole story for a very long time. But I knew that you, Mother, would be worried because of Grandfather. If he had suspected what might happen, the shock could have killed him. As it is, I believe he died happy and what I have to say can no longer harm him."

Ruth gave her head a little shake. "What I propose to do is nothing very terrible, nothing you haven't done yourselves." A brief smile lit up her face. "You see - sometime next year - I hope to be married to John McCarroll. And Mother," she added quickly, "nobody is going to make us change our minds!" Ruth now looked anxious, as she hurried on: "John wanted to tell you both about us the day he came here to say goodbye. But he, too, decided it would be better to wait."

Leah and Ray stared wide-eyed at their daughter. "Well, Ruth - this has been quite a shock," Leah said. "I think you should have told us sooner, dear. Nobody here would have tried to make you change your mind. I do understand your concern for your grandfather, but he did not have to be told."

Leah's thoughts went flying back to those terrible days when her father had learned of her own friendship with Ray. And she had felt so guilty wounding someone who had reared her with such thought and concern for her welfare.

Ruth had kept her secret well, even knowing her own father could not be displeased at the turn of events. And, of course, in the present climate of bitterness between certain sections of their two religious groups, Ruth and John must feel they would be happier away from their troubled land, especially when John had a job to go to.

Ray said: "We never imagined it would be you and John. We always thought you would settle down with Robert. But we like John, too."

"Poor Robert," Leah said. "So this is why you have treated him so casually over the past two years?"

"Oh, Robert knew about John," Ruth said. "He has known for ages. Robert and I were always the best of friends, that's all. Now he has Caroline and I believe they are soon to be engaged." Ruth looked quite relieved that all had been explained at last.

Then she continued: "John is home for a few days. We came over together. He intends to see you at once before we return." Her eyes held a fondly amused look as she added: "To ask for my hand in marriage! You see, he's just like Daddy, very old-fashioned, courteous and kind - and I love him very much." Her voice broke and she stared wordlessly from the window.

Leah glanced at Ray who, like herself, seemed deeply moved. "We can only feel glad that both of you are so happy," she said. Memories were stirring. Ruth must never suffer as she had suffered from parental opposition.

"Of course, we'd like to come back here to live as soon as possible," Ruth said hopefully. We love this country. It means too much to us to want to leave for ever."

"I'm glad to hear you saying that," Ray put in. And Leah could see he was beginning to realise the significance of what they had been told. He gave Leah a thoughtful look. He, too, was fully aware of the difficulties that would lie ahead for their daughter.

"And please don't worry about our different religious backgrounds; John and I will work something out." She smiled at Leah. "After all, I'll have an advantage over mother - I'm already used to living with members of the Catholic church." Her eyes rested affectionately on her father. "And it hasn't been too difficult!"

Ruth got up to leave. She looked radiant. "As you can guess, I now have a very important 'phone call to make."

"Tell John we hope to see him tomorrow," Leah said.

Ruth smiled her thanks and disappeared quickly.

Ray stood up, and his eyes showed a brightness Leah could well understand. "Well, now," he said, "Ruth certainly had something to tell us!" His look changed. "But you must be disappointed, Leah?"

She shook her head. "How could I be - when Ruth is obviously so happy? And I have always liked John." Then she fixed her eyes challengingly on Ray. "I've just remembered something! You told me, years ago, that you would advise any daughter we might have to do what her mother had done - and marry a fine young Roman Catholic!"

"And you see what has happened," Ray said. "Ruth didn't need any advice; she knew what to do herself!"

Yes, Leah thought, Ruth had simply chosen someone she felt she could be happy with. Her religion, like Leah's, was something she felt strongly in her heart. It had no special name; it vied with no other beliefs.

Ray pulled her gently to her feet and, for a few moments held her close.

"Please don't worry about them, Leah. We have managed so far, haven't we? They will, too, in their own way. And now, before I see Patrick and get on with the work, I'd better call at the bungalow and tell them the news. Mother, of course, will be pleased. And Stephen, too, when he comes tomorrow."

Left on her own, Leah wandered into the front garden and sat on the old wooden seat in the fading sunlight of the late August evening. At least she felt happy knowing that Ruth and John would never be barred from their parental homes and made to feel they were outcasts as she herself had been. She could only pray that the outside world would also show them some understanding. It was sad to think that bitterness and hatred could come from those on either side of the community who professed to have strong, religious beliefs.

Leah looked up and saw Ruth approaching.

"John will be here tomorrow afternoon," she reported in some excitement. As she came on and sat beside Leah she looked a little more subdued.

"Mother - I didn't plan for this to happen," she said, "any more than you did when you fell in love with Daddy."

"I know," Leah answered. "We are, all of us, only human. And man-made rules and beliefs should not divide us. I've been

179

wondering, Ruth, if you'll remain a Protestant?"

"You did, Mother, didn't you? Anyway, where we are going no one seems to worry much about what religious beliefs you have or if you have any at all."

"I wish it could be like that here," Leah replied. "But what really matters, Ruth, is the kind of person you are and how you treat others. Too many people here keep remembering events of the past and making certain friendships impossible."

"Yes, I sometimes worry a little about the future," Ruth confessed. "So does John. I know you and Daddy had many difficulties to deal with. But you both kept our home happy. Any unpleasantness we experienced came from outside."

Leah gazed across the fields towards the river where the current was running strong after heavy rain of previous days. She thought how beautiful, fresh and peaceful the countryside was looking. It seemed impossible that killing or bombing might be taking place somewhere in their land at that very moment.

She watched a mallard drake flying swiftly along the line of the water towards the boggy ground upstream. It was safe for the moment. But, after the first of September, the guns would be out again - making every flight a hazard.

Leah felt a deep sadness, knowing that many people had to face a similar risk every day. Would it ever end?

As though in answer, a sudden biting wind came sweeping down the valley.

"I think we should go in," she said, getting up quickly. Recent events had been a big strain. She felt tired out.

But, as her rather thoughtful-looking daughter joined her, she said, brightly: "I want you to know, Ruth, that I feel quite happy about you and John. You have different religions, but they are just patterns of worship that have evolved over the centuries. Unfortunately, these differences are the main cause of our present Troubles. But you and John have a sound basic faith on which to build your lives."

Ruth nodded, and gave a hopeful little smile.

At the door, Leah said: "We're going to miss you very much, Ruth. But I'm sure you'll come to see us whenever you can. And now I must 'phone Helen and Muriel and tell them all our news."

180

TWENTY-ONE

When Ruth and John had returned to England, Leah felt a strange blankness in her life; all her hopes and plans for her daughter's future had come to nothing. Two of their children had now left home and gone their own chosen ways. Yet she was conscious of a certain satisfaction in this thought. Had not she herself done the same? But she closed her eyes recalling the heartache of her own home-leaving, the years of worry that had followed and, above all, her feelings of guilt over the suffering of her parents.

Now times seemed to be changing - slowly but steadily. More people than ever were showing tolerance, friendship and understanding between the two cultures. She recalled her recent talk with Helen and Sean and felt sure they were genuinely pleased that their son, John, was to marry Ruth. Helen had confessed that she had guessed early on that this might happen.

Life on the farm was continuing much as usual. And throughout the province, periods of quiet, happy days were still being shattered by further news of death, suffering and destruction - often involving both the guilty and the innocent. Then, for a time, all would be peaceful once more.

Over at the Coulter farm, Muriel was getting ready for her daughter Anne's marriage to a young businessman in the city. Leah was often called on for help in the preparations.

Then, just days before this happy occasion, Ray's mother passed away quietly in her sleep. Ray 'phoned Ruth and Stephen and they arrived the next day. Leah felt that old Mrs Anderson, who had found much happiness through her family, had died content believing that Ray's children, too, had turned out to be all that she would have wished for them.

The mourners at her funeral included many Protestant

neighbours. The cars gathered along the main road and then covered the two long hills on the approach to Ray's church - moving slowly behind the hearse with its flower-laden coffin.

Ray's mother had left all her affairs in order. The farm had already been signed over to Ray after the birth of his two sons. Now, in her will, she had bequeathed money to her church and to her children. Leah had been surprised and touched to know that the old lady's china and jewellery were to be divided between herself and Louise. She was also happy to know that Louise and her husband were to remain at the bungalow until their new home was built. These days, she and Louise often set off together to visit the family cousins in the country, or they drove to the city to see Leah's mother and then on to the coast to call with Aunt Emily.

Letters came regularly from Ruth and Stephen. Ruth now had a permanent teaching post and her last letter had announced: "John and I hope to be married very quietly in the summer before coming home to see you all." Leah wrote at once wishing them every happiness and success.

Stephen would be home, too, and happy to see them. Reading his letters also showed her how dedicated he was to the priesthood. And Ray, like his own mother, was immensely proud that one of his sons hoped to become a Roman Catholic priest, to give his life completely to the work of their church.

Lately, they had been seeing less and less of Patrick in the evenings. He was working well on the farm, but now he had a special girlfriend, who lived out in the country some distance away.

"I'd like to bring Roisin to see you. Would next Sunday do?" Patrick asked, one evening as he was preparing to leave the house. He looked at Leah with a rather worried expression.

"Of course, Patrick," she answered quickly. "We'd love to meet her."

But he still appeared uneasy. Then he sighed. "Mother - don't be offended - please. You see, Roisin hasn't had much social contact with Protestants. And the few she has met - well - she didn't like them very much."

"Look here, Patrick," Ray put in. "I bet there are one or two Catholics around she wouldn't like either. You bring her along. She has nothing to fear from your mother."

182

Patrick frowned and shook his head. "I know, I know - I've told her that. It's just the way she has grown up - never having had a chance to really know any Protestant people." With a look of embarrassment, he hurried away.

Roisin, when she arrived, was a slightly built young girl of medium height, pretty, with short, dark hair and hazel eyes.

"She's just a slip of a lass and she's probably feeling shy," Ray remarked. Now from the sitting-room window, he and Leah saw the two young ones strolling in the front garden, chatting and laughing together.

"Well, she didn't look and talk like that with us, no matter how I tried to put her at her ease," Leah remarked. "And she scarcely ate anything - after all my special efforts at cooking! But I suppose she'll get used to us in time."

"So you really think they're serious about each other?" Ray asked.

Leah nodded. "Oh, yes. Patrick has never brought home any other girl, except Roisin."

Ray's eyes widened as though on a sudden happy thought. He reached out and took Leah's hand in a warm, strong clasp. "I brought home only one girl, too - remember?"

A host of memories swept over Leah. And Ray, she thought, had never changed. "Well, that's what you tried to make me believe!" she said, laughing. "Anyway, Patrick appears to be very happy with Roisin. He has known her for some time, I believe. She's a farmer's daughter, one of six children. I really think they will soon be announcing their engagement."

When Roisin had left to be driven home by Patrick, Leah and Ray discussed the possibility of their being married in the near future.

"Well," Ray said, "Louise and Dermot hope to have their new home finished and ready by next summer. When that happens, Patrick could begin married life at the bungalow, as we did. And I hope he and his bride will be as happy there as we were."

On Leah's next visit to Belfast, she was surprised to find her mother confined to bed and looking pale and drawn. Aunt Emily had already arrived and was busy in the kitchen.

"I was just feeling very, very tired," Leah's mother said. "I don't know what came over me. It must be this colder weather. I'm well looked after, you know, and now it's very comforting to have Emily staying with me for a few days. She even called the doctor! He has given me tablets and says I must stay here and rest."

Two days later, Leah was shocked to hear that her mother had died suddenly during the night. She was nearly eighty-five.

"Poor Margaret," Aunt Emily said. "Her heart just gave up. I'm going to miss her very much."

Once again Leah was back for a short time in her childhood home, back among the memories of her early days and those more recent happenings that had so upset her. Always, she would remember her mother's kindness. Against great opposition, she had tried so hard to stand by Leah during her years of marriage.

Ray and Patrick joined the few friends who attended her mother's funeral to the country church, where she was buried beside her husband Matthew. "She did all she could for us," Ray said.

The bungalow in the city was now Leah's and, after removing a few precious mementos, it was let for a year to a young couple, friends of Helen and Sean.

Soon it was the beginning of another year at the farm. And Leah and Ray had made plans for an evening out to celebrate their wedding anniversary. Torrential rain had fallen for nearly a week and Ray and Patrick had been digging drains and putting in pipes near the house to deflect the terrible flooding away from the yard and the outhouses.

They were finished on the afternoon of the party and Leah, at the kitchen window, saw that Ray had brought out the car and was hooking on the trailer. Then he threw in a roll of barbed wire and a few wooden stakes.

"Surely you've done enough heavy work for today," Leah called. "It will soon be dark and we don't want to be late tonight."

Muriel and Tom were to call for them and then drive to the city to join Helen and Sean.

"Some of the cattle away at the out-farm have been seen on the road," Ray explained. "Patrick was told about them. He drove them back this afternoon and put bushes in the gap. But I'd like to make a more secure fence. An hour or so should do it. Don't worry; I won't be late." He waved and drove off.

Leah did a few jobs about the house and, as the daylight began to

184

fade, she laid out their best clothes and made preparations for their evening out. Patrick had been doing the milking. And soon she heard him closing up the cattle and fowl. She was beginning to feel a little anxious and wondered what was keeping Ray.

Then, at last, she heard a car approaching at some speed and she hurried to put on the kettle. Ray would be ready for a quick cup of tea. But it wasn't Ray.

Disappointed, she watched as a car turned quickly at the yard gate, lifted Patrick and raced away into the darkening night. Well, he couldn't be going far or he would have told her. But someone was in a big hurry. Maybe a neighbour in need of a helping hand in an emergency.

But where was Ray? It was over two hours since he had left. The house seemed very quiet now and full of shadows. Reluctantly, she switched on one or two lights. It had been easier to watch from the window in the darkness. She kept glancing at the big kitchen clock and listening. She didn't usually worry like this; Ray was often delayed by one thing or another. But tonight was different. She began to pray that he would be kept safe, that he would come soon.

And then she heard another car - pulling up at the front this time. But there was more than one car! Had Patrick arranged some little surprise for Ray and herself? She ran to put on more lights and to open the door. As she gazed into the night, she was conscious of hearing subdued voices. But suddenly they faded into a strange silence.

Now she saw Patrick coming slowly towards her. But she scarcely knew him. His eyes looked dark, his face pale and strangely twisted. She heard him sobbing and her heart sank as he put his arms around her.

"Oh Mother, Mother - poor, poor Dad. Just remember he did not suffer. It was all over very quickly. But why, why should it be our poor Dad?"

Sad-eyed people were around her now. Louise and Muriel, weeping, led her into the house. She heard broken, whispering voices trying to comfort her. But she could not believe that Ray was dead, caught in cross-fire between the security forces and armed men. None of this was real. It could not be true. Then - something was happening to her. Someone was holding her - and everything was growing dim . . .

"You fainted, dear," Louise said, as Leah moved to sit up. "Just sip this drop of brandy." Her voice was an unsteady whisper.

For Leah, the days that followed all seemed part of some terrible dream. She moved about the house helping silently with the daily round of things. Louise and Dermot took charge of all the arrangements. And Patrick, too, was grateful.

Leah wept when Ruth and Stephen arrived, and when Ray's body was brought home. Soon the house was full of relations and friends. The priest was there and the minister from the village church, both deeply shocked by the tragedy and trying to bring some comfort to the family.

When they all knelt for prayers before the coffin left the house, Leah broke down again. Soon another large Anderson funeral was wending its way to the church on the hill.

Leah felt deeply moved by the Requiem Mass: the prayers, the incense, the ringing of the bell, the sprinkling of Holy Water. Today, it all had a special significance for her. The altar boy leading with the crucifix, others following with lighted candles, the priest saying prayers - this was for Ray who had harmed no-one, but who had been cruelly taken from them.

Many mourners spoke quietly to Leah, pressed her hand and shook their heads in bewilderment as they offered their condolences. Leah thought of the many people of her country who had been ruthlessly murdered or crippled. She remembered other families who had lost fathers, mothers, children - and those whose homes had been destroyed. She herself still had her health and her family. But how utterly cruel life could be, how difficult to understand.

That year went slowly for Leah. One thing that helped her was the news that Louise and Dermot would not be moving from the bungalow for quite some time. The work on their new house had been held up by storm damage and flooding. Muriel and Helen were also constantly in touch with her.

Then, shortly after Christmas, Roisin and Patrick were to be married. Patrick was now the owner of the farm and it was only right that he and his bride should live at the farmhouse. Ray had made his will following his mother's death. All the family had been remembered. And Leah also had right of residence at the farm or bungalow, as she so wished.

The excitement of the wedding gave Leah a new interest. Everything went very well with Roisin's family and all the gathered guests.

But she was a little worried about her relationship with Roisin when they were living under the same roof. She longed for Ray to be there to help her make friends with this young girl who, through her upbringing in a different religious community, was finding it difficult to accept Leah's friendship. Not only was Leah from a tradition outside Roisin's experience, she was also her mother-in-law.

When Patrick brought his young wife home after their honeymoon in Paris, Leah did her best to be unobtrusive in the house and yet helpful when it seemed necessary. But sometimes she felt she was doing and saying the wrong thing. Often this caused periods of silence between them, or Roisin would shut herself away until Patrick came home.

But Patrick, who had been so close to his father, appeared to need Leah's help and advice on many matters to do with the farm. At other times, she felt she was in the way of the young people who, naturally, wanted to live their own lives.

Louise kept telling her that time would improve matters. But Leah was not prepared to wait. Other plans were forming in her mind. Her mother's house was now empty. She would go there for a time and see how she felt about the future. She recalled her early days of marriage and her happiness with Ray in a home of their own, despite disapproval from some quarters concerning what was called their 'mixed marriage'.

Roisin, trying to adjust to her new way of life, would be happier on her own with Patrick. She was bound to feel lonely at times and often disturbed when people appeared to be breaking all the rules and enjoying friendship with members of 'the other side'. But Leah knew that Louise would help Roisin to understand that this was both right and desirable for the peace and happiness of their country.

That evening, after supper, Leah spoke of her plans to Roisin and Patrick. She said that Ray's death remained very fresh in her mind and she was still seeing him everywhere.

"So - I think it would be better for me to go away for a while."

Patrick's eyes widened in alarm. He tried to say something. But Leah stopped him. "I should like to stay for a time at my old home in the city," she said. "I have lots of things to see to there before I re-let the house."

"But Mother - you can't go off on your own!" Patrick put in quickly.

"It's what I want to do," she told him. "I'll be all right. I'll have Helen and other friends quite near. Then, when Louise and Dermot are settled in their own place, I'd like to come back to live at the bungalow here."

Leah knew that the countryside, so loved by Ray and herself, and all the people who had shared their lives, would always call her back.

"In the meantime," she added, "you're not to worry about me at all."

"We - we'll come to see you in the city," Roisin said quickly, and glanced a little nervously at Patrick as she lifted dishes from the table.

"Of course, Mother - of course we'll come to see you, often." Patrick still looked stunned by her announcement.

Leah moved towards the window and stood gazing out across the fields where Ray had worked so hard. How difficult it was not to remember other days and to dwell on what had happened. But she must not think of those things now.

She turned and said, quietly: "I know I'd be lost away from Muldare for any length of time. I belong here, now."

Patrick came towards her. "Mother - you must come back as soon as possible. We'll have the bungalow painted and everything ready. And before that, you must come to see us - and keep us right about the things to be done for your return."

"Yes," Roisin said, nodding in agreement. Their two flushed faces regarded Leah anxiously.

"Oh, I'll be here to see you all," she told them. "And I'll certainly look forward to my return to the bungalow." She smiled then and left them.

Yes, Leah thought, the bungalow - with all her memories - was where she wanted to be.

THE END